I0580033

Reagan Through the Looking Glass

BOOK ONE IN THE HACKING WONDERLAND SERIES

ALLYSON LINDT

For my eternal dragon

Chapter One

Wayne Dickinson nearly always sounded like he was on the verge of panic. Though he was on the other end of the line, his out-of-breath ranting told Reagan he paced as he spoke.

"You need to find a way out tonight." He'd be ringing his hands or peering out the window through the blinds. "Rent a car— *No.*" She heard the blinds snap shut. "Don't do that. You'd have to use a credit card. Fuck."

Every time he cried *wolf,* Reagan jumped. Not today. "And changing my flight requires ID. Oh. I could use an internet cafe, bounce my signal a few times, and schedule a series of Ubers from here back to there. It would mean driving all night, but it would make me difficult to trace." As she talked, she wove her way through the crowds at the Cesar's Palace convention center.

"That's brilliant."

"*Wayne.* I'm not doing that." She couldn't keep the exasperation from her voice. When they were in class or in front of other students, he was *Professor Dickinson,* but he insisted on *Wayne* whenever professionalism wasn't required. It was one of the reasons she liked having him as a thesis adviser—he didn't care for unnecessary formality.

That appreciation was offset on days like today, when he gave into rampant paranoia. "This is real. It's not a hunch. I'm not imagining things. You and I need to get off the grid today. We can figure out the details once we're out of harm's way."

When she started working with Wayne, she freaked out every time he did. Someone was trying to kill him, was stalking her, was monitoring all their text communications—the list went on. Nothing ever came of it, and he was never able to prove his suspicions beyond *I just know*. It probably came with the territory. As a digital-security expert, he had a scary grasp on those things that went *bump* in the virtual night.

It was why she sought him out in the first place, but she wasn't going to become him—the conspiracy theorist with the aluminum hat, who thought the government was monitoring their every word. She was going to remain normal for as long as possible.

"I'm staying here." She paused outside the exhibit hall, picking a spot away from the exit. "There's a day left."

"*Alice*." He called her that because she was chasing Jabberwock. If he was using it now, it was meant to remind her she was dealing with someone who was unstable enough to call themselves Jabberwock.

She rolled her eyes. "Tell you what—I'll turn off my phone as soon as I hang up with you. That way, no one can trace my signal, and I'll be impossible to find for the next twelve hours." They both knew that wasn't an effective solution, but it would keep him from calling her back.

"No—"

"See you tomorrow." She disconnected, powered off her phone, and dropped it in her purse.

Like him, certain pieces of data impacted her decisions and direction, but she let determination drive her forward rather than push her into a corner. The only way to find her answers to what had happened to her brother was to dig into the dark and terrifying. This trip was research mixed with pleasure, and there was no way she was calling it off early because Wayne decided now was an appropriate time to go on high alert.

Alex always accused her of letting desire and a thirst for that next rush of adrenaline override common sense. Maybe he was right, but it hadn't been an issue to date.

She strolled into the hall. *Where to go first?* She'd been through multiple times, but each trip she found something new. As she wandered the aisles of booths, Wayne's warning gnawed at her thoughts, the way his paranoia always did. What if this was the one time he was right? The answers she searched for—what she claimed was her thesis research— were tied to more than a few illegal markets. Not that she was doing anything outside the law, but her target had his fingers in anything and everything most people preferred to keep secret.

She was following the trail of Jabberwock. The Keyser Söze of the deep web. It was rumored he could connect anyone, if they could pay his price. But that was all it was—rumors. There wasn't any proof he was more than a name people used when they wanted to conduct illicit business. He was that well digitally hidden.

Reagan knew he was real as surely as she knew she was in Las Vegas. He'd killed her brother. More likely had Alex killed, rather than pulling the trigger himself, but Jabberwock was at the center of it all.

For five years, she'd been looking, and had found hints here and there that brought her closer, but she could never quite crack through to Jabberwock's identity. When she met Wayne in a conspiracy theory forum, it took her years to develop a bond of trust. When she reached that point where he was willing to share his real name, she went out of her way to apply for the Master's program at the school where he taught.

She worked with him under the premise of him being her Master's thesis advisor. The paper and degree were real, but her motivation behind both weren't what they appeared in her records.

The paper's purpose was to show that digital communication—phones, texts, the internet, and even the deep web—could never truly be secure, because people weren't perfect. Even the most cautious, highly trained individual let something slip.

Wayne was already obsessed with Jabberwock. She didn't need to nudge him toward it, and with his help, she found a trail that pointed to something other than rumors.

She wasn't sure yet what she'd do when she

found Jabberwock. The bold, brash part of her thought maybe she'd shoot him. Alex had taught her how to use a gun, and she was good. But not cold-blooded-killer good. She still had a conscience. One thing was certain—she was going to ask Jabberwock *why Alex?* Her brother might have made some missteps, but he didn't deserve a fate like having his life taken so early.

She shoved the rambling thoughts aside. If she followed the path of what Jabberwock was capable of, she'd dive headfirst into Wayne's panic.

An urban legend of an internet kingpin didn't care about a Master's student from Utah. She should enjoy the technology in front of her and learn what amazing advances had been made in internet security.

She approached a booth displaying a hardware solution that promised new and unhackable levels of encryption and compression. The one thing these companies never considered was that it didn't matter how difficult it was for a computer to crack your data, if you accidentally gave your identifying information to the stranger on the train. Not that most people had to worry about that. Some of the most paranoid individuals didn't have data worth stealing.

"Excuse me." Reagan tried to catch the attention of one of the two men working the display. They might as well be clones. Identical jackets, ties, and haircuts, but one was a brunette and one blond.

Tweedle-Blondie glanced in her direction, then turned back to his tablet.

"I have a few questions about your product." She spoke in a distinct, firm tone.

Tweedle-Dee looked her up and down. "I'm with someone else. I'll be with you in a minute."

Reagan clenched her jaw. She wasn't sure which part of her appearance made this difficult, but she suspected her torn jeans, and Wonder Woman T-shirt didn't scream *big money*. Make a scene, or go look up the information she wanted online? What were the odds these two could answer her questions, anyway?

"What do you think?" a male voice asked.

When no one answered, she whirled and realized a guy was looking at her. And—holy fuck— he was hot. Dark hair trimmed short, and a suit that hugged his body like it was made for him. Maybe it had been. She didn't know a lot about expensive suits, and usually their owners put her off, but the hint of tattoo above his collar and the way he studied her with piercing green eyes made her willing to stash the prejudice.

"Me?" Wow. That was less than brilliant. "About what?"

"The product." He nodded at the booth, a hint of a smile tugging at his mouth. "Worth it?"

"Good afternoon." Tweedle-Blondie stepped up next to them, hand shoved toward the new arrival. "I'm Jake, and I'm happy to answer any questions you have about our hardware."

Reagan's irritation surged back up, but it vanished quickly when Suit-Guy kept trained his gaze on her, ignoring Jake and his greeting. "Well?" Suit-Guy asked.

"I'd skip it." She was being a little spiteful, but there was honesty behind her response.

"We can talk over here if you'd like." An edge crept into Jake's voice.

Suit-Guy turned his back to Jake, which brought his shoulder to rest against Reagan's. "Why?"

She couldn't hide her smile. "If it's anything like their previous version, it's a Meraki imitator, with some older compression and a back door that leaves it vulnerable to war drivers."

"Bullshit." Jake spat the word out.

Suit-Guy finally looked at him. "Oh? So you've fixed those issues, then."

"They never existed. Our hardware VPN is solid and top of the line."

"I'm sorry, this isn't going to work for me." Suit-Guy shook his head. "I expect you to lie to me about your product, but this young lady knows what she's talking about, and I won't abide the rudeness."

Jake's face flared red, and he narrowed his eyes at Reagan. She shrugged and turned away.

Suit-Guy fell into step beside her as she meandered down the aisle.

As soon as they were out of earshot, she gave him a grateful glance. "Thank you."

"You had it under control. But I am curious about something."

"What's that?"

"Why were you waiting to talk to them if you already knew?" he asked.

The question made her pause. She knew the answer, but not the right way to phrase it. She didn't mind pissing off Tweedle-Dee and Tweedle-Blondie, but Suit-Guy was nice scenery. She'd like to enjoy his company a little longer. "I wanted to know…" She sighed. Might as well lay it out all plain-like. "The latest version has the flaws too. I wanted to know what language they'd use to spin its shortcomings. If they'd paint it as a feature or unnecessary, or something else." Because buzzwords that covered flaws were as much a part of her thesis as anything.

"That makes sense." He chuckled. "Are you liking anything you see, or is it about finding the holes in their offerings?"

"Both. Nothing's bulletproof, but there are a few new products that come closer than in the past." Normally she didn't talk like this with anyone except Wayne and some of her classmates. It made her come off as arrogant and cynical. She was just practical.

The way he looked her way every few seconds, focused on her and not something past her, made her feel as if he was genuinely interested.

She liked the attention and that he could keep up. "I was looking at Glommettech and their firewall. Did you check that out?"

He was close enough his arm brushed hers with each step.

They were halfway down the next row, before she admitted to herself she was more focused on that and him than on the exhibits. "It's good stuff. I'd have to poke it a little, to see what they're not saying, but I was impressed."

Their wandering took them away from the booths and toward the exit. She should thank him for his time and head back in. Walking away from the crowds with a stranger was a bad idea on the best of days, and with Wayne's warning hanging out there, it seemed borderline irrational.

It also rushed through her veins with temptation and the promise of something more-than-ordinary.

It didn't hurt that she swore a spark flowed between her and Suit-Guy.

"Watch it." He wrapped an arm around her waist and pulled her closer, as a hotel employee barreled in the other direction, pushing a refreshment trolley. His grip was firm, possessive, and oh-so tempting. And abruptly gone. "Didn't want your toes to get trampled." He nodded at her sandaled feet.

Considerate, observant, and intelligent. He was almost too good to be true. What was the catch? If there was no catch, there was no risk, no fun, and no reward.

They turned another corner and followed a path around the outer edge of the hotel lobby.

"I have a confession to make," he said.

And there was the catch. "Oh?'

"I've seen you around, the past couple of days. You kind of stand out in a crowd."

He'd been watching her? Wayne's panicked warning raced back and her pulse kicked up another gear. It wasn't fear that gnawed her gut, it was curiosity. "I'm not sure if that's creepy or flattering." It was only creepy if the attraction didn't flow both ways, right?

"A little of both, I'm sure." His words were an eerie echo of her thoughts. "But it's not what it sounds like." He was leading her toward a lower-traffic part of the convention center. "You're the one person I've seen here who understands what people are selling and knows enough to see through the hype. And I'm hoping to get your opinion about hardware." He nudged her into an empty room.

Odd place to have a conversation about hardware. Unless he wanted to show her his. Definitely out of the ordinary. Logic told her she should be on alert, but fuck, Alex might have been right—her drive for thrills may get her in trouble tonight.

The abrupt notion flared scorching through her veins. Suit-Guy didn't emit any sort of warning signal though. Reason said walk away, but her instinct trusted him, and the war inside heightened her desire to see *what next*. She shouldn't be turned on by the idea, but God help her, she was picturing his broad shoulders under that jacket. What he'd look like shirtless. Those cool, pale eyes trailing over her naked body.

And she wasn't above a little prompting, to see if he was interested in the same. "Is that a thinly veiled euphemism? Some kind of weak pick-up line? *Come back to my room, and we'll see if my hardware fits your wetware.* Or *I bet my dongle would be a perfect fit for your socket.*"

The only problem Reagan had with casual sex was that sometimes finding it was more difficult than she'd like. Her last roommate was horrified to learn Reagan didn't do relationships, but that kind of emotional attachment was another thing that got in the way of her search. Of her goals. Sometimes a girl wanted more to get off with than her vibrator, but Reagan liked brains with her dick, and that seemed to be a tough order to fill. This guy offered enough of both to intrigue her.

Okay, that was an understatement. In her mind, she was lying naked under him, moaning in pleasure as he stretched her out.

He raised his brows. "Tell me you've never heard lines like that." Disbelief peppered his statement.

"Once or twice."

He backed her against the wall, a few feet from the door, and the scent of spice and musk filled her senses. His breath was hot on her cheek. "If I was propositioning you, you'd know." Despite his low voice, she heard the deep tone loud and clear. "I'd say something like, *how do you feel about leaving these stuffy suits behind, heading back to my room, and letting me fuck you until you can't walk?*"

That's a big promise. Sure you can deliver? That was what she *wanted* to say. The words lodged in her throat, as her imagination took off on its own. With as close as he stood, body pressed to hers, she could feel the size of his... promise, digging into her hip. Tempting. Filling her head with images of his hands roaming her body. Heat flared across her skin everywhere the fantasy touched, until her nipples strained against her bra and need pulsed between her thighs.

"In case you were wondering"—his words rolled over her—"*that* was the proposition. You interested?"

There were more holes in his story than the security system the Tweedles were selling, but she'd been talked into bed by less, and she had no illusions that this was more than a random fling in a hotel room. The thrill of it raced through her, mingling with lust and anticipation. Seemed like a fantastic way to spend her last night in Vegas.

She grabbed her composure and flashed him a smile. "Definitely."

Chapter Two

He kissed along her neck. "Is this where you insist you're not this kind of girl?" His question caressed her skin.

"I'm definitely this kind of girl." Reagan tilted her head, to give him a better angle. "If you're looking for a weak protest wrapped in morality, you're going to be disappointed."

"I'm not worried about being disappointed." He drew his hands up her sides, thumbs on her ribs and then brushing the bottom of her breasts.

She arched her back into his touch, and her nipples hardened, aching for attention. Voices drifted in from the hallway, louder than they should be. Neither she nor her sexy stranger had closed the door. Anyone could walk in on them. The realization pulsed between her legs.

He yanked her shirt over her head and traveled his mouth her collarbone and down the middle of her chest. When he kissed along the top of her breast, she dragged her nails down his back, trying to pull him closer. Needing *more*.

A laugh caused her to jerk her head toward

the exit.

"Worried about getting caught?" he asked between licks over her skin.

She was terrified, but that made the arousal more intense. "Hoping they want to watch." She found his erection and traced the impressive outline through his slacks.

He pressed against her hand, gyrating his hips each time she stroked. What would it feel like, to have him buried inside her? He pushed one breast from its cup and lowered his head to her nipple.

When he flicked out his tongue, she whimpered and shifted closer. He nipped at the swollen bud and she groaned. She swore for a moment that the sound outside vanished. It returned, full-volume, and her heart started up again.

With a quick flick, he undid the button on her pants, and dipped his hand under the elastic of her panties. He continued to suck her nipple, as he stroked along her slit, then dipped toward her opening and slid two fingers inside.

She bucked her hips, and he pulled out to move back up. He found her clit, and she gasped. The attention on two different fronts drew her close to climax, pleasure building inside.

She crashed into orgasm, grinding against his hand, until his touch was too much and she jerked away.

He brought his mouth down on hers, their lips crushing together as he hooked his thumbs in her waistband. The fervor of the moment raced through her, making her forget the wobble in her legs. He shoved her jeans and panties to the ground, then spun her toward the wall.

Fingers knotted in her hair, he tugged her head back. "I need to fuck you." He nipped her earlobe and her neck.

She wiggled her ass against him. She heard the tear of foil followed by the sound of a zipper, and seconds later, he yanked her hips to him, glided the head of his cock along her slit, and plunged inside her.

"God. You feel good." Did she say that out loud? Fire tinged her cheeks. She'd never been a dirty talker before.

"It helps that you're so wet." He withdrew to the tip, before thrusting again. "Fuck, you're tight." With one hand on her stomach and the other on her hip, he pulled her into his torso, while he kept a steady rhythm, slamming inside her and hitting just the right spot.

Orgasm built again. She bit her tongue, to keep from screaming, as ecstasy crashed over her. She clenched around his cock, pressing back into him, and floating into the clouds as the moment drew on.

His grunts and short, hard thrusts told her he was close too. He ground against her as he came, gripping her tight, and pounding for several seconds before he slowed.

Her thoughts swam, blissfully clear. As the endorphins faded, her legs wobbled, and the voices outside surged back to tease her.

Wow. What a rush.

Reagan rested her forehead against the wall, content to let the sound of them catching their breath be the conversation. She should cover herself before someone walked in on them. As soon as her limbs felt like moving.

"What are your plans for the rest of the night?" His question sent shivers of conflict down her spine.

She liked hearing him talk. She really liked the idea of a round two in bed. She had zero interest in forming an attachment, ever and especially to someone who picked her up at a tradeshow hundreds of miles from home. "I, uh…" if she was going to turn him down, she'd rather put some distance between them, than be half-dressed and way too comfortable leaning back into him.

The air kicked on, and cold rushed over her, raising goosebumps in its wake. That added to the topic of conversation seemed like a good reason to tug on her shirt and pull up her pants. She nudged him back and stepped away from him, to dress.

He let her go without resistance. "Don't misunderstand. I know what this is," he said.

She met his gaze. "No names. No numbers?"

"Right." He stared back, unflinching. "But my night's open, and I enjoy your company more than mingling with a bunch of salesmen who aren't telling me the whole story. My proposal is this— we'll order dinner, test out the giant tub, and see what else we can get up to before we go our separate ways in the morning."

"I have to admit that sounds like a decent arrangement."

He gripped her waist and pulled her close. The heat of his body chased away the chill of the room and sank into her bones. He trailed his nose along her neck. "What do you say we head upstairs and see where the night goes from there?"

He was offering to buy her dinner, keep her company, plus more of what had the potential to be incredible sex.

She was good with that. Better than she should be. "Five seconds. Or ten." She turned on her phone long enough to send her roommate a text that said *Met a hottie. Call 911 if you don't hear from me by morning.* Reagan clicked *send,* powered off the device, and looked at Suit-Guy. "I'm in."

When they got back to his room, they skipped the tub in favor of something quicker, and spent their time in the shower, getting clean then filthy. She had to put something on, to keep from flashing the porter who delivered their meal, her mysterious-but-sexy Suit-Guy draped his shirt over her shoulders. The way he looked at her, as though she were the main course, made her pulse race.

They tested out his jetted tub in what became a drawn-out tease session, fucked in bed, and fell to the mattress tangled around each other.

Definitely not what she expected when she started her day, but an evening she'd keep fond memories of and revisit often—no doubt—for a long time.

When she woke up the next morning, she was alone in the room. As she cast her gaze around, an unfamiliar stone sank in her gut. It wasn't just that he was gone, but so were all of his things. There were no suitcases. She scrambled to her feet and checked the closet.

Empty.

Like the counter in the bathroom. Her clothes were folded on a chair, her purse on top, with her phone and wallet untouched inside. At least he didn't rob her.

Something caught Reagan's eye. A note scribbled on hotel stationary sat next to the TV.

Alice,

Her blood ran cold, and she sank to the mattress before her shaking legs gave out on her. Only Wayne called her that.

Had a blast last night. Sorry to run before you woke up. I was late. Check out of the room when you're finished.

Hatter

PS-Turn on your phone.

If she was freaked out by his knowing her nickname, *his* name turned her skin to ice. What the fuck did she step into?

She grabbed her clothes and yanked them on with shaking hands. The rip in the leg of her jeans tore when she accidentally jammed her foot through the worn fabric. *Fuck fuck fuck.* Tension surged inside. She shoved her bra in her purse and pulled her shirt on.

As she walked into the hallway, she turned on her phone. The more distance she put between her and his room, the more her pulse slowed. It was probably a stupid thing to get all strung out over, but the note left a bitter taste in her mouth.

Wayne hadn't left her any more messages—which surprised her—but there was a voicemail from her roommate. As she stepped onto the elevator and pushed the button for her floor, she let the message play.

Mindy's voice drilled into her thoughts. "Reagan, I need you to call me. I don't want to do this over the phone, but you need to know. Professor Dickinson is dead."

Reagan let out a half-sob, half-gasp, and her shaky legs buckled. She slumped back against the wall of the car. Terror, grief, and nausea raced through her, stealing the strength from her limbs, and Wayne's pleading echoed in her head.

It was a coincidence. It had to be. This wasn't related to his paranoia last night.

It didn't matter how long she mentally shouted the insistence. She didn't believe it.

Chapter Three

Reagan glanced over her shoulder every few seconds between the elevator and her room. There was no one there, but that didn't slow the hammering of her heart against her ribs.

Landlines are safest. Don't trust anyone. Wayne's voice echoed in her thoughts. She fumbled with her keycard before sliding it into the lock and pushing the door open.

She bolted both latches the moment she was inside, and clenched her hand into a fist, to keep it from shaking. She wasn't going to surrender to paranoia. This was a coincidence. A horrible, tragic…

Grief surged inside, and she swallowed hard.

Everywhere she looked, shadows jumped out at her. Something moved on the wall, and she had to clench her teeth to keep from squeaking in shock. *Just the sun reflecting off my phone. I need to chill.*

She tossed her purse on the bed, grabbed the hotel phone, and dialed Mindy.

"Hello?"

"Hey. It's me." Reagan forced her voice to stay calm.

"Hey." Sympathy lined Mindy's tone. "I didn't recognize the number. Did you get my message?"

"Forgot to charge my phone. Listening to your voicemail took the last of my juice." It was easy to spit out the lie when her mind was splayed in a million spots at once. On top of the news, the creepy note from her one-night stand taunted her. *God*, how could she be so stupid? She didn't know how Suit-Guy—it stung less to think of him that way, than by the name he left on the note—was related to this, but his finding and distracting her last night was too convenient.

"Reagan?"

Shit. She missed what Mindy said. "Beg pardon?"

"Everyone on campus is freaking out about this, but you and Dr. Dickinson were close. How are you holding up?"

"I don't know. Not well?" Reagan sank to the edge of the mattress. She didn't trust her legs to support her long enough to pace. "What happened?" *Freak heart attack.* That would be it. Or he choked on a hot dog. Aneurysm?

"Depends on who you ask. Some are saying suicide. I went by his place, being nosy for your sake, and all that. That big bay window out front is shattered. I'm thinking the people who say it was a burglary gone wrong have it right. Either way, Major tells me it was a gunshot." Major was Mindy's boyfriend and worked for the coroner's office.

And *bullet wound* sounded as ominous as it got. "Fuck. He told me this was going to happen. He called me last night and tried to warn me, and I brushed him off, and I didn't—"

"*Stop.* You swore you wouldn't get sucked into the spooks he saw hiding around every corner. This has to hurt, but don't let it tear down your reason."

"Right. You're right." She wished she could be as rational about this as Mindy. Reagan had an idea of what kind of people hid in the shadows, though. "I'm shaken up, but you make a good point."

"Good. Catch your flight, come home, and we'll get blasted drunk tonight. Help you work through this."

Reagan smiled at the phone, but it didn't ease the ache inside. "Good call. I'll see you this afternoon." She hung up.

As she packed her bags, she let Mindy's logic play on a loop in her thoughts. By the time she checked out, sorrow had muted anxiety. She headed to her rental car. She passed through the lobby and something caught her attention out of the corner of her eye. *Suit-Guy?* When she whirled, it was just three business men jabbering, heads bowed together.

Don't jump at shadows.

The drive to the airport was short. Check-in and security moved quickly. Less than an hour later, she was waiting at her gate. She grabbed a book from a gift shop. She had several on her phone, but that stayed in her purse, powered down.

Every third word, her attention drifted from the page as she glanced around the airport. A familiar suit caught her attention, and she whipped her head in that direction. Nothing. She was being ridiculous. Even if it were him, he wouldn't be wearing the same suit today unless he'd spent the last of his money on it.

She needed to focus on the story she was reading. Vampires, demons, and lots of hot sex—perfect distraction.

A loud *bang* ratcheted through the room. Reagan screamed and dropped her book. Anyone not looking at the woman whose suitcase had fallen and broken open, was staring at Reagan.

Heat flooded her face, and she did her best to hide behind her paperback. By the time her flight boarded, she was jumping at everything and still didn't understand the first paragraph of her book.

She scanned every face on the way to her seat, trying to memorize them, and continued to study the people who boarded after her. Once the plane doors were closed and it taxied down the runway, she found enough calm to unclench her fists and roll the kinks from her neck. It wasn't a state of Zen by any stretch of the imagination, but she managed not to make a sound when the cart in the center aisle broke free, rolled to the back of the plane, and clattered against the wall with an ear-splitting *crash*.

As the flight reached cruising altitude, more of her tension faded. With thirty-thousand feet between her and the ground, she could grasp more of the calmness that normally kept her from getting sucked into conspiracy theories. For as many times as Wayne cried *wolf*, last night was coincidence. A horrible, tragic one, but still coincidence. As the stress ebbed, sorrow knotted in her chest until she couldn't breathe.

She was grateful she was in an aisle seat. She fumbled with her seatbelt and rushed to the bathroom. Inside, she bolted the door, leaned back against it, and sobbed. She sank to the floor and pulled her knees to her chest. Tears spilled down her cheeks, as she let sadness wash over her. He'd been a good friend, and as over-the-top as he was, he looked out for her.

When she had herself under control, she splashed water on her face and returned to her seat.

The plane landed without incident, and her drive home was the same. The next few days passed in a blur of condolences while the university scrambled to find her a new thesis adviser.

Thursday afternoon, she scanned her thesis research and writing to date, to cement the highlights in her mind, and she sat down with Dr. Dunlop. Reagan didn't have any classes with the instructor, but rumor was the woman was practical and fair.

"I've read over Professor Dickinson's notes, but to start, I'd like you to tell me in your words what your thesis is about."

Reagan could do this. She'd memorized the elevator-pitch version before she even started the project. "Advances in digital security are made every day. However, as long as human beings are an access point to that information, there's no way to make it one-hundred percent secure. Through an examination of technology and human nature, I'd like to show where the weak points are, and why their existence is not a terrible thing, as long as we recognize it."

"Good, good." Dr. Dunlop nodded, as she

scanned the tablet in front of her. "I do have one concern about your research."

Reagan's enthusiasm slipped. "I'm sure I can address whatever you're seeing."

"It says here you've been tracking a Jabberwock. That's his name, not what he is?"

"That's correct. As possibly the best-hidden figure on the deep web, he made a perfect case study." She spoke with confidence, despite the odds the advisor was about to tell Reagan this was a wild-goose chase.

"I see. So Dr. Dickinson let you chase imaginary people."

And there it was. "Not imaginary. Private."

Dr. Dunlop set her tablet aside, steepled her fingers, and looked at Reagan. "I've read some of your essays and looked at your academic record. You're intelligent, and you excel in your courses. Professor Dickinson was the best at what he taught, but he saw conspiracies around every corner. I don't know that the best use of your research hours is falling down a rabbit hole, to find an invisible man who supposedly is some sort of Godfather of the internet black market."

"I don't—" Reagan bit the inside of her cheek, to keep from blurting out something she'd regret. Even if she didn't buy into Wayne's various paranoias, what she was looking for existed. But phrasing that the wrong way wouldn't leave a good impression.

"Ms. Lidell, it's been a tough week for you. Before you respond, take a few days to think about it," Dr. Dunlop said.

"I'm sorry—what am I thinking about, exactly?"

Dr. Dunlop's smile wilted at the corners, and pity lingered in her gaze. "Whether or not this topic is the best use of your time. Your initial theory is sound, but consider whether you might be better served with a new proof."

"I'm satisfied with what I've chosen."

"As I said, give it a few days to simmer in your head." Dr. Dunlop stood and gestured to the door. "I have other meetings. Enjoy the rest of your day."

Reagan let herself be ushered into the hallway, struggling to grasp the right protest. Where was she going to find anyone else with the same kind of experience as Wayne? She could adjust her thesis, but it wouldn't change her desire for answers about Jabberwock.

The viewing and funeral were on Saturday. The chapel was crowded with former and current students, as well as staff. Wayne might have been paranoid, but he was also a good guy, liked by most people who knew him. She let her attention trip over faces, some familiar and others not. She stalled on a man in the back row. His blond hair was pulled into a ponytail that fell past the collar of a black suit. Even seated, it was clear he was tall and slender. His face, chiseled and handsome, stole her thoughts and made her stare.

He met her gaze, hazel eyes boring through her, and she jerked away as heat flooded her face. What was it about him? He didn't look like he belonged here, but she couldn't say why. He also seemed familiar, in an eerie way that clung to her memory but didn't shake anything loose.

Whispers rolled through the room as everyone took seats in the chapel.

"Such a wonderful man... can't believe he's gone."

"...a bit off his rocker, though..."

"...conspiracy theories... nutty... hope he's finally at peace."

At the wash of doubt and gossip, Reagan clenched her jaw until it ached. It was worse that the eulogy contained a lot of the same.

She wanted to stand up in the middle of the church and scream that these people had no idea what was going on in the world around them. Men in shadows making deals and deciding fates with no checks and balances.

"Hey. You all right?" Mindy nudged her.

Reagan yanked herself from her head and looked around the room. People were filing toward the exit. She must be extra distracted, to not realize it was over. "I'm good."

"Are you up for the cemetery?" Mindy studied her, concern lurking behind her gaze.

Reagan nodded and fell into step beside her roommate. They reached the church steps, and she spotted a man leaning against a tree, across the street. *Hatter.* Her stomach dropped into her shoes, and she stopped.

"Watch it." Mindy tugged her arm.

Reagan moved out of the flow of traffic and whirled to face the people behind her. "Sorry." She looked back over her shoulder, and he was gone.

"What's up with you? Is it just the funeral or something else?" Mindy asked.

"Nothing. The funeral. School." Reagan's thoughts weren't on the conversation. She searched their surroundings but saw no sign of him. But she hadn't imagined it this time. It wasn't a trick of light or her overactive imagination. Even from that distance, she swore she'd felt his pale eyes boring into her. An afterimage of him had pressed itself on her thoughts.

Mindy pursed her lips. "Okay. Should we go?"

"I'll meet you there. I need a little time. Please?"

"I get it. Catch up when you're ready."

Reagan surveyed the church grounds from her spot at the top of the stairs, as the procession thinned. Then, there was no one else around but her. She didn't see Hatter. He hadn't simply vanished. Where did he go?

"Reagan Lidell?" An unfamiliar male voice greeted her, and a hand rested on the small of her back. "I didn't think I'd find you alone. It's a pleasure to finally meet you."

She whirled to find herself face-to-face with Ponytail-Man from the church. "How do you know my name?" It wasn't the politest thing she could have led with, but whether he was handsome or not, his lead-in had her heart grinding against her ribs.

"I know a lot more about you than you realize."

The stranger's greeting did the opposite of calming Reagan's thoughts. The way he approached her—the familiarity in his tone—combined with the events of the last week sent adrenaline spiking through her veins.

She broke away from his touch and headed toward the parking lot. "I'm sorry." She didn't look to see if he followed. If he could hear her. "I need to catch up with my friends."

"Can we go someplace quiet and talk first?" He matched her pace.

"I'm going to the cemetery."

"I assumed you would. We can regroup after, if that's better for you."

She paused and turned to face him. "It's not. No meeting is better for me, since I don't know you and have no clue who you are. Go away or I'll scream."

"I just want to talk."

"And I just want an island in the Pacific." Reagan forced sarcasm into her voice to keep her fear from shining through. "I don't know you. I don't like that you approached me alone. My friends are waiting for me, so leave now, or I'm calling the police."

He held up his hands. "Introductions come with talking. Leave if you'd like, but I'm following you anyway."

"Great. At least you're honest about the creepy." She resumed her path to her car, quickening her step. She wanted to sprint, but wouldn't give this persistent asshole the satisfaction. Besides, it was hard to run in these shoes.

"I was asked to keep you safe."

That a random stranger thought she needed to be kept safe added a new spark to the churning inside. "If I'm concerned that's an issue, I'll go to the police." She was impressed with herself, for keeping her voice from cracking. She reached for the car.

He stepped in her way, eyes flashing hard and cold. "And if you do, you'll be dead the moment you walk out of the police station."

Ice slid through her veins. "Who are you?"

"A friend."

A harsh laugh slipped out. It was better than a sob. "Bullshit, you are. You threatened my life."

"What?" His eyes grew wide, and he moved out of her way. "No, I... Oh. I guess I can see... I didn't mean it to come out that way. I'm an acquaintance of Wayne's. I'm here to help you vanish off the radar."

"I've got it covered, thanks." Something new caught her eye. Her front tire was flat. "Are you fucking kidding me?"

"Do you keep the spare and jack in the

trunk?"

On any other day, at any other time, under any other circumstances, she'd probably be flattered at the implication he was going to change the flat for her. "I've got it. Thanks." As she spoke, his gaze drifted toward the trees at the far end of the church parking lot. "Excuse me?" Could she drive this thing any distance as it was? If she walked to the nearest convenience store, would he follow? Maybe heading back into the church was her best bet. "I can see you're busy. I'll be on my way.'

"*Shh.*" He didn't look at her.

Her irritation spiked, pushing aside fear. "Hello?"

He grabbed her wrist and yanked her down next to him as he dropped into a crouch. He covered her mouth and locked his gaze on hers. "I'll be clearer." A growl cut through his whisper. "Shut the fuck up."

And here was anger. She preferred it to the fear that wanted to resurface when she tried to break his grip and couldn't. She raised her other hand, and his eyes hardened.

"Stop." The way he said the word rolled down her spine like freezing water. "Someone out there is watching us. Watching *you*, I suspect."

Hatter?

"Everyone else is gone," he continued. "If I pull my hand away, you're welcome to scream or rant or whatever the hell it is that gets you off, but only I and whoever is out there will hear you. Do you understand?"

She nodded. What else was she supposed to

do? In her head, she calculated if she could sprint to the church or the convenience store faster. In the church she could bolt the door. Call the police. Hide.

She started to rise the moment he let her go. An ear-shattering *bang* ripped through the air. The window next to her head exploded, glass shards flying everywhere. A scream tore from her throat without permission.

Did someone just shoot at her? Was it Hatter? Instinct took over, propelling her away from the stranger. She pumped her legs as fast as she could, sprinting across out in the open asphalt, eyes on the chapel doors.

"*Reagan*," the stranger called after her.

She pushed so hard, her calves burned, but she was at the steps. A few more seconds, and she'd be inside.

Someone tackled her, and she skidded to the ground. Gravel got embedded in her shins. The stained-glass window next to her exploded with the sound of another gunshot, distracting her from the pain.

"*Stay down.*" Ponytail-Man held her in a crouched position. He wedged the church door open a few inches and pushed her inside.

Another shot, and the wood above her head splintered, spraying both of them as he followed her into the building. Keeping a tight grip on her arm, he half-led, half-dragged her toward a confessional booth and pushed her in. He squeezed in next to her.

"Keep your fucking mouth shut," he said, voice so low, she barely heard him over the hammering of her pulse in her ears.

She nodded, not sure she could speak if she wanted to.

He reached for something under his jacket. When he pulled a pistol from a concealed holster, her heart threatened to tear from her chest. Seeing a gun drawn while she was under fire was on a different universe from shooting one at an indoor range. What the fuck was going on?

A *creak* carried from the front entrance, and through the curtains, she saw the shadows move and shift.

Ponytail-guy raised his gun, and she bit the inside of her cheek, to keep from whimpering. *Please don't let anyone get shot.*

The front door clattered shut, and she heard a muffled, *"What?"* from outside, followed by the crunch of shoes on glass. "Yeah... Running.... Should... she's... All right. I got it." It wasn't Hatter's voice. The realization wasn't any comfort.

And then, there was nothing. Or maybe she couldn't hear over her screaming pulse. Seconds ticked away, and tears stung her eyes, while bile burned her throat.

"Don't move." Ponytail-guy mouthed the words as much as said them. "Will you listen to me this time?"

She didn't even know if she could make her legs work. He might be the only thing holding her upright. She nodded.

He moved the curtain aside to slide from the booth without a sound. She strained to hear. Through a gap she saw him move along the front wall, under the windows, gun ready. He raised his head to peek through the glass, then ducked again. He pushed open the door a crack, then straightened and stepped outside.

Was he gone? How long until he came back? She should run, but fear froze her muscles. She willed herself to move. To get the fuck out of Dodge.

The curtain ripped open, yanked from a direction she couldn't see, and her heart lodged in her stomach.

It was Ponytail-Man.

"It's safe now." He held out a hand.

Her mind was done working. She accepted the offer of help and let him pull her into the room. He looked her over, gaze lingering on her legs. realized glance down told her they were covered in scrapes and dried blood. So the pain wasn't all fear.

"Are you all right?" he asked. Concern replaced his sharp tone from moments earlier.

She shook her head.

"Will you let me take you someplace safe now?"

"Who are you? I don't even know what to call you." She still didn't trust him, but he wasn't the one shooting at her, so he had that going for him.

He gave her a tight-lipped smile. "Hare."

Another recurring character from the Wonderland books. She choked off her laugh before it could become a sob. "That's not funny."

"It's not meant to be. I don't know why they left, so I don't know if we're safe here. Can we go?"

"Okay." She didn't know what else to do. The sarcastic bit of her pointed out that if she wanted to find Jabberwock in his digital Wonderland, she had to follow the white rabbit. She argued with her sarcasm that this was March Hare, and White Rabbit was an entirely different character.

He pointed her toward the back of the building and led her out a rear exit. With each new step, as fear turned into numbness and adrenaline ebbed, the ache in her legs grew.

In a parking lot across the street, he helped her slide into the passenger seat of a battered Honda sedan.

He took the driver's spot and started the engine. He looked at her. "I, uh… I knew your brother. Alex always spoke about you like you were at the center of his universe."

She clenched her jaw, and a whimper escaped through her teeth. "Bullshit."

He studied her, brow furrowed and concern in his eyes. "He used to call you Ray. Too bright for your own good?"

The familiar, teasing jab sank into her bones until her joints ached. Alex did do that, and as far as she was aware, no one but he and Reagan knew that.

"Trust me long enough to get you out of here?" he asked.

"But as soon as we're safe, you explain what's going on."

He didn't say anything else on the short drive, and she didn't ask. She had no idea where to start, without sending her thoughts spiraling out of control. They pulled into the back lot of a motel, and he let her into one of the rooms. If she had to guess, she'd say he paid cash for this place. Probably didn't have to show his ID or prove who he was in any way.

No one would have any idea where he was, even if they'd seen her with him. The thought should terrify her, but given that she'd been shot at, anonymity sounded like an acceptable risk.

"Have a seat." Hare pulled a chair from the desk, gripped her fingers, and helped her settle in. "We need to clean up those scratches." The threat was gone from his voice, along with the arrogance and assumption. Only kindness lined his words.

"Okay."

He dug through a black duffel bag next to the bed, and a moment later produced a small pouch. He set that aside and vanished into the bathroom. She heard water running.

Her thoughts swirled with the sound, as she tried to make sense of what happened. She couldn't.

He emerged a moment later with a washcloth and knelt at her feet. When he brushed the loose gravel from where it her skin, she clenched her jaw and hissed. When he pressed the hot washcloth to the open wounds, a gasp tore from her throat, despite her efforts to the contrary.

"I'm sorry." He looked at her, sincerity shining in his eyes. "I'm trying to be gentle."

"I can tell." She hadn't been this scraped up since she was a girl. Her mother was forever getting upset with her, for the spills she took on her bike and the multiple pairs of jeans she ruined in the process. All to keep up with Alex.

The memory of him clenched like a fist around her heart, and she bit back a sob. He'd always been there for her, and now...

"Did that hurt?" Hare asked.

"No. It's fine." She used the sharp sting of his cleaning her wounds to stay grounded in the present.

A few minutes later, he stood. He grabbed some clothes from his bag and handed them to her. "If you'd like to shower and change, that will rinse away the rest of the grime. We can figure out how to get you supplies of your own, after."

She stared at the offering. "I'm not... No. Tell me what's going on—who just shot at us and why you're here—then take me home."

"That's fair." He sank onto the mattress, putting several feet between them. "You already know who shot at you. Or at least, who ordered it."

"No." It didn't matter that she spent years pursuing Jabberwock. That she was certain he was responsible for Alex's death. And Wayne's. Something about having bullets fly past her head put the entire thing in a context that was too vivid and real.

"I don't have proof it was Jabberwock, but odds are good. That's what's going on. Whoever came for your professor wants you next. I'm here because Wayne asked me to extract you from the situation if anything happened to him. He always felt bad about putting you in the middle of his manhunt."

"That's too simple." She didn't mean to say that out loud.

He arched a single brow. "Really." His tone was flat, but still kind. "You'd rather I spun a wild story around it? I'm CIA Black Ops, and this is a safe house. You're here because you unwittingly downloaded the plans to the secret weapon Canada plans to use, to destroy the world, now that we think they're a benevolent country."

She laughed in spite of herself. "I'd kind of prefer that. Yes."

"Why?"

"Because then I'd seem more reasonable when I wouldn't believe you. You don't even have a real name."

"Trust goes both ways. I promised to look out for you, not tell you all my secrets."

That made sense. Like everything else he was saying. "But why *Hare*?"

"It's the game we're playing." The casual way he spoke called to her doubt. "There are a lot of people who want to know who Jabberwock is. I'm talking on an international level. He has ways of finding us, the way he did Wayne. The names keep our real identity out of things, and they're a way of making light of an otherwise dangerous situation. For instance, Wayne called himself Walrus, correct?"

"Yes."

"And he called you…?"

Alice. The answer died in her throat. Because she didn't want to be the arrogant one who assumed she was the center of the story? "Reagan."

He frowned, but it vanished again so quickly, she might have imagined it. "He never did want you sucked in too far."

"Why didn't he ever mention you?"

"Why didn't you ever tell him about your brother? We all have our secrets."

She never told Wayne about Alex because she didn't want him to know her search was anything beyond academic. This Hare guy had too much information. Enough to terrify her as much as it persuaded her to hear him out. "How do you know Alex *and* Wayne?"

He leaned in and looked her in the eye, elbows resting on his knees. "When Alex died, I did my research on the angel of a little sister he adored, and you're not as well hidden as you think. It led me to Wayne and discovering he and I had a shared interest in Jabberwock. If I can find this much about you, so can anyone else. You don't have to give me your blind trust, but I need enough cooperation to keep us both alive."

That made sense. An eerie amount of it. "I'm here, aren't I?"

He handed her the stack of clothes. "Change into something more practical. Wash off the dirt. Lock the door and bar it, if you're worried about me. Use the time to think this through, and then we can talk about next steps."

She didn't have a reasonable argument. "All right." She took the T-shirt and sweat shorts from him, and locked herself in the bathroom. She forced herself through the motions of stripping down, turning on the water, and stepping under the stream.

If she paused for even a moment, and looked at the situation as a whole piece, she'd collapse in fear and indecision. Despite not having an answer to *what next*, she knew surrendering control wasn't it.

Standing under the hot water and letting it sluice over her body gave Reagan a chance to organize her thoughts. Tension thrummed in her veins, but it didn't have the same edge to it as before.

She didn't trust this Hare guy. Had no proof or reason to believe he was who he claimed. For all she knew, he worked for Jabberwock. Or was CIA Black Ops. Or… The possibilities were endless.

However, he hadn't killed, hurt, or even really threatened her, and he kept her from getting shot. On top of that, she needed information. More than ever, she had to get close to Jabberwock. She didn't know what she'd do when she found him, but she'd figure it out along the way. He was responsible for the deaths of at least two people she cared about, and she wanted to find out *why*.

If Hare had any information that would help in her search, it was worth sticking around. She'd be cautious and examine anything he said. She could do that.

She stepped from the tub and stared at her

reflection in the steam-fogged mirror. A blurry her stared back. Wild red locks fell around her face in wet strands, further distorting the face watching her. It was no more surreal than the rest of her day.

The clothes Hare had handed her were loose on her. The T-shirt hung halfway down her thighs, and the shorts passed her knees. Which made sense—he was five or six inches taller and a bit broader in the shoulders compared to her slight frame.

She forced another round of *you've got this* through her head, unlocked the door, and stepped back into the main room.

Hare sat on the bed, back against the wall, as he flipped through TV channels. He had the sound turned down and the subtitles on. He stood the moment he saw her. "Feeling better?"

"Much. Thank you." She couldn't help giving him a second look, now that her mind was clearer. He'd shed his suit coat, leaving the shoulder holster—complete with pistol—on display. The implied threat didn't detract from the fact he was attractive.

Shit. She reached for her purse. "I told my roommate I'd catch up with her. I need to let her know not to worry about me." Reagan grabbed her phone.

Hare shot his hand out and grabbed her wrist before she could blink. He pressed a tendon hard enough she dropped her phone into his waiting hand. "Are you kidding? You've still got this on you, *and* you think it's okay to use?"

"Really." Indignation sparked inside Reagan. She was as irritated with his condescending tone as with the voice inside that agreed with him. She knew better, but the terror of the day threw her reason out of whack. "I'll turn it off, then."

He clenched his jaw. "Battery can't be removed without breaking it. I *should* destroy it."

"That's a six-hundred-dollar device." Not that she paid that much. Her job barely kept her current on bills. The phone was a gift from Mindy, when she upgraded to the newest generation. The train of thought reminded her about work. If this Hare guy got pissy about her checking in at home, what was he going to say when she needed to leave, to get to her job?

It was a ridiculous train of thoughts, given her afternoon, but she struggled to wrap her head around being shot at. That it happened to *her*. That it was real.

He pulled a padded envelope from one of his bags and dropped her phone into it. "We'll go out later tonight or tomorrow morning, and you can call her from wherever we end up."

"You're as bad as Wayne. Am I a prisoner now?"

"Nope." He handed her the envelope and stepped back. "You're welcome to leave whenever you want. I'll even give you cab fare."

She hesitated, waiting for the catch.

"This is sinking in for you," Hare said. "I get that. It's tough to accept the implausible, even if you know it's true. I'll lay this out from my perspective, and you can decide if you want to stay."

"Okay...?"

"You've got the attention of a powerful man."

Hare settled onto the edge of the bed again. "I'm not talking US-Senator or Saudi-prince powerful. Jabberwock is the man who holds their secrets, and when needed, their leashes. He conducts his business digitally, because he knows how to hide in that world. For whatever reason, you've made it your goal to find him and wrapped that in the excuse that no one can truly hide online. If that's true—if you're right, and he's spent years lying low—do you really think he won't find you first? Especially if you do things like using your cell phone and talking openly with your new student adviser about him."

The ice was back in her veins, thanks to not only his tone, but also the tiny details he seemed to know. "Of course I considered all that." She forced herself to laugh. To pretend his mini-lecture didn't terrify and humiliate her. In reality, knowing the threat was there and believing it were two separate things.

He sighed and stood. "Someone followed you to a funeral, waited until you were as good as alone— no witnesses—and tried to shoot you. You never saw the guy. If I were in your shoes, I'd call Mindy and tell her you'll be gone for a while. That you're visiting a long-lost relative out of state, or whatever she's going to buy. Tell your boss the same thing. Resign yourself to the fact that you're not going back to that life, and figure out how to move forward. Embrace the fact that you've got someone with you who has your back—that's me, by the way—until you're ready to vanish completely. But that's just what I would do. You can still walk out the door and go home."

The deluge of reality overlapped what lingered in her thoughts, and she sank into the nearest chair. "I'll do it your way."

He gave her a tight smile. "I'm sorry to be the bad guy here, but this isn't a pampering situation. I'm going out, to grab us some essentials. If you're gone when I get back, I'm writing you off. Don't let anyone in, regardless of what they say. Oh—and what size do you wear?"

"What?" She stumbled on the question and stared at him. "You mean you don't know? You've got the rest of my personal details on mental file."

"I only know what I can find online. I don't care if you're a two or a thirty-four; I figured you'll want something to wear out that isn't mine."

He knew a little more than what she talked about online, because she hadn't even told Mindy about the conversation with her new student adviser yet. She stowed that curiosity for later, suspecting he wouldn't give her a straight answer. "I'm an eight. Tall, because long legs."

"Great. I'll be back in two hours, tops."

She didn't move for a while after he left. This new world continued to settle around her. Sickness churned in her gut, but the fear ebbed. She grabbed the remote, but nothing on TV caught her attention. Reality shows felt trite, police procedurals were dramatic for the wrong reasons, and the sitcom laugh-tracks drilled into her head until she thought she might vomit.

At what point did she step through the looking glass, into this world, where rampant paranoia was both the norm and the only thing that might keep her safe?

Time passed more quickly than she expected. She couldn't calm her racing thoughts, though. Every sound from outside made her jump. Each new smell required she analyze it. Was this smoke? Should she be worried about that *thud*? Was the temperature rising in here? All her senses were on high alert.

When she heard keys scrape against the lock, her stomach dropped into her shoes. Frantic, she looked around the room for something to use as a weapon, in case it wasn't Hare. She grabbed the phone, the only heavy thing that wasn't bolted down, and backed up against the wall.

When Hare stepped inside, she relaxed with relief. He raised an eyebrow at her makeshift weapon, then set several bags down at his feet. "At least you took me seriously."

"You made a convincing argument." She set the phone back on the nightstand. The nausea, coiling tension was back full-force, knotting her gut and neck.

"I wish I didn't have to." He handed her one of the bags. When he shifted the purchases, the smell of fried food greeted her, making her sick and reminding her she hadn't eaten all day. "Something to wear, until I can take you shopping. I'm sorry if I came off as harsh, but this isn't the kind of situation you fuck around with."

"I get it." She grabbed the offering and looked inside. Jeans, a T-shirt, and a package of panties. There was also a cellphone he probably picked up for ten bucks at a convenience store. He was right; it would do.

"Use the phone to call anyone who's going to be looking for you, and tell them you're safe," he said.

Right. Cut herself off from her life. "I'll be back." She stepped into the bathroom to put on the underwear, and make her calls. Mindy was sympathetic when Reagan said her grandmother has passed way, and she was going to be gone for a few days at the funeral. Mindy told her to take whatever time she needed. Her boss wasn't so forgiving. He said not to bother coming back when she was done doing whatever she was doing, and hoped she was keeping a list of all these *deaths* so she could come up with new ones as excuses at the next job.

When she returned to the main room, Hare was taking food from a paper bag and setting it on the desk. "Hungry?" he asked.

Never eat it unless it's pre-packaged. Alex's voice echoed in her head. An odd warning from ages ago, that he'd drilled into her and she never understood why.

She shook her head, and her stomach growled in disagreement. "Yes, but no." She raked her fingers through her hair, but dropped her arm back to her side when her hand shook.

He closed the distance between them and grasped her fingers. "How are you really doing?"

"I don't know." She was still hyper-aware of everything. His touch seared her skin. His scent drilled into her thoughts, both tantalizing and taunting. His voice sent chills down her spine, and she swore she could taste him. "Afraid, but not?"

"It's adrenaline." He stood so close she saw

the flecks of dark gray in his eyes, like shattered ice. "Once you calm down a little, it'll fade, but it's going to make you sick unless you burn it off."

"I'm not much of a treadmill girl." Her chuckle sounded hollow to her own ears. "Not that they'd have an exercise center in this place. And I have a feeling going jogging is out."

He glided his palms up her arms, raising goosebumps along the way, and cupped the base of her neck. "If I were a sleazier kind of guy, I'd try to convince you sex was the best way to burn off the excess energy."

Her breath jammed in her throat. The suggestion raced through her, igniting desire and doubt. She liked it more than she should. The idea of being pinned beneath him. His hands roaming her bare skin. Her diving into his kisses. God, she was fucked up if she was thinking about sex at a time like this. Enjoying the rush was one thing, but what the hell was wrong with her?

She licked her lips. "But because you're not?"

"I'm going to tell you the next best thing is a good meal, a better night's sleep, and finding your center." He stepped away.

She was relieved—and nothing else—that his solution was simple. There was no disappointment at all that he dropped the sex conversation, because that would be ludicrous, given the day she'd had and how little she knew about him.

Telling herself that didn't quell the thrum of desire that took his suggestion and let it set up fantasy-time in the corner of her mind, but she managed to mostly ignore that.

Chapter Six

Reagan leaned against the counter near the motel-room coffee maker, while the last drops sputtered into the pot. She grabbed one of the disposable cups from the stack next to it, poured half of the dark liquid, and added generous portions of cream and sugar. She looked at Hare, whose attention had alternated between her and the door since she woke up. "How do you take yours?" she asked.

"I don't do the coffee thing." Last night, he insisted she take the bed while he kept half an eye on their surroundings. When she woke up, he was dozing in a hard-backed chair. His eyes shot open the moment she stirred. It was both reassuring and disconcerting, but that described ninety-nine percent of interacting with him.

"How do you survive without caffeine?" She kept her tone light and teasing. "Did you even sleep?"

"Knowing what's out there tends to keep me on my toes." His tone was flat.

She sipped her coffee, not caring that it

scalded on the way down, to cover her lack of a response. When he didn't reply, she perched on the edge of the overstuffed chair by the bed and searched her thoughts for a new subject.

Sitting around here for the next few days or weeks, or however long he deemed was *safe*, didn't seem like a great idea. That might be a good topic to bring up. If she had an alternative.

"I need to find you someplace safe for the next few days." His comment startled her.

While it was what she wanted to hear, after his lecture last night, suspicion crawled through her. "Why?"

"You're not my life. I'm sure you're a great person and all that, but I have other responsibilities."

"Like what? Or does that fall under *Information you don't Trust me with*?"

"It does."

It made sense, but that didn't sate her curiosity. His suggestion to relocate her raised another question. "Does that mean you'll stuff me in a different room for a few days, no contact with the outside world, and then vanish until you feel like it's time to come back for me?"

"Do you want to stay out of danger?"

"I want to not go out of my mind with boredom." She wasn't answering his question, but she was being honest.

He sighed, and his expression softened. "It's only for a few days. You're not going to die of boredom in that amount of time. Besides, what I have to do is dull. For instance, do you see yourself as a wine-tasting kind of person?"

The question triggered a memory that flitted just out of reach. She focused and grasped for it. Right. Wayne had been planning on attending a wine-tasting tomorrow. In the midst of death and chaos, she forgot. One of Jabberwock's men was supposed to be there, checking out a potential client before the next step in whatever business deal they had.

She wanted to be there. "As a matter of fact, I do see myself as a wine-tasting person."

"You're not."

The hint of disbelief in his voice raised her ire. "What's that supposed to mean?"

"What do you think it means?"

She wouldn't give him the satisfaction of answering; that argument wouldn't suit her purposes. "If you're attending some sort of affair that gets you closer to Jabberwock, I'm going with you." Not that she was in a position to make demands, but she had to do *something*.

"If I was going to that it would be the kind of event you have to fit in at. If you stand out, you'll blow everything."

It was a bunch of people sitting around, sipping fermented grapes, and talking about how woodsy or nutty the different glasses tasted. She couldn't fathom it would be that hard to blend. "I can fit in."

"Have you ever seen one of those awkward-teenager, coming-of-age movies?" Hare asked. "I'm talking Anne Hathaway style. Nerdy, unpopular girl finds herself immersed in high-class society, because *contrived plot*?"

"I guess." She didn't like the implied comparison.

He sighed and leaned in, elbows resting on his knees and gaze locked on her. "There's always at least one scene where the spunky heroine is plunged into the middle of a high-class event and embarrasses herself—dinner with the prince, or dancing at the country club. At the time, everyone cringes, but by the end of the film, everyone accepts she's quirky and fun and her way of doing things is the best way."

"Yeah…?"

"Real life doesn't work that way. This is an invitation-only event, and if you so much as sniffle in the wrong way, you'll draw attention to yourself and there won't be a fun *happily ever after*."

She couldn't comprehend any social situation that was that uptight. "I can behave. You can't keep me locked up for the next… however long you've got in mind. I was hunting down this man before you came along, and I plan to finish. This is the best way to make sure you and I don't step on each other's toes."

He pinched the bridge of his nose, and seconds dragged by without him responding. "You may be the most poised person in the world, and that won't matter if you don't do everything exactly right. If you go with me, you have to promise—swear on your life, because it's that serious—to take my cues and do everything I tell you, when I tell you. You don't argue and say you know or you think it's stupid or any complaint you have. Don't be offended. Don't decide this event is your chance to shine and be unique. To blend in, you'll do what I say."

"I promise." She would have sworn to do almost anything, if it meant getting her back on track with her search.

He stood. "Then we need to update your wardrobe. And dye your hair. That red stands out a mile away to anyone looking for you. How do you feel about becoming a blonde?"

"The blonde could be fun. But shopping? I don't have a lot of money in my bank account. Less, considering I quit my job." Not that she wanted to talk him out of this, after taking the time to convince him to let her go, but she didn't know if she could afford a five-dollar latte, let alone formal eveningwear and a dye job.

"We're not going to the mall, so it's not as though you'll be wandering around in public, and the outing is on me."

"I can't owe you for something like this. How do you make an offer of this magnitude without hesitating? In fact, how are you paying for any of this? What's in it for you?"

"Another one of my secrets, I'm afraid." He gave her a smile.

Twenty-four hours ago, a look like that might have been enough to talk her out of her panties. It was still seductive, but it also made her blood run cold. It seemed as though he had more secrets than truths, especially considering what he knew about her.

Hare opened the back door to a brick building and gestured Reagan through before falling into step beside her. A wash of scents greeted her, spicy, sweet, and a rainbow in between. It washed away the lingering chemical smell in her sinuses—a reminder she'd spent the last two hours in a salon, having the color and identity stripped from her hair and replaced with blonde.

Her mouth watered, and her stomach growled with the reminder that the only food she had yesterday was greasy pizza, and her breakfast was coffee.

He held out his arm, and she looped her hand through at the elbow. He led her toward a podium and told the host they wanted a table for two in the back. They were led toward an unoccupied corner of the restaurant.

She tried to take in her surroundings without staring, as they passed through the room. White linen draped over the tables. The smattering of other diners were dressed more like Hare than Reagan—the men in slacks, button-down shirts and suit jackets, but without ties, and the women dressed in blouses, slacks, and skirts. Reagan wore the department store clothes Hare brought her last night.

They reached their table, and Hare held out her chair, then scooted it in as she sat. He took the spot across from her. She looked around the room again, before turning her attention back to him.

"Are you all right?" He sounded concerned. Every time he looked at her, a tender concern hid behind his gaze.

"I thought we were going dress shopping." She kept her voice low, not wanting to disrupt the ambient quiet of the room.

"I'm not doing a fantastic job of keeping you safe if I let you starve. Is that's all that's bothering you?"

She leaned in. "I feel a bit underdressed." That was an understatement

He covered her hand with his. The simple gesture sent a blanket of comfort through her. "And you were trying to convince me you'd be fit in tonight without help?"

"I was grasping." Her laugh came out shaky.

He scooted his chair closer and leaned until his mouth was near enough to her skin his breath warmed her cheek. "Fuck what they think," he whispered. "You look comfortable. Gorgeous even. And I'm not just saying that. Compliments about appearance have consequences."

"Thank you." Heat flooded her cheeks, and she was grateful for the dim lighting. "I know you're trying to keep your secrets, but you know so much about me. There's got to be something I'm allowed to ask you."

"There are a lot of things. What do you want to know?"

She didn't expect him to give in so easily. "Um… how old are you?" It was a starting point.

"Thirty-two."

Only seven years older than Reagan, but it might as well be a lifetime, for how he handled life compared to her. "You're so experienced."

"I suppose I am." He laughed.

She nodded at his chest. "That thing"—she didn't want to say *gun* out loud in a public place—"you have strapped to you—do you know how to use it?"

"We'd both be fucked if I was carrying it and didn't know how."

"Touché." She tried to keep her tone casual, despite the way his answer made her heart hammer. "Can I have one? I can use it. That is, I'm into this deep, right? Or you wouldn't have yanked me away from my life." She still didn't know if she would, if it came down to it, but she wanted to believe she'd act, rather than being shot.

The waiter interrupted. "Are you ready to order?"

Hare looked at Reagan. "May I?" he asked.

She felt enough out of sorts that letting him order for her might be easier than deciding if she should ask for anything other than the cheapest thing on the menu. "Please."

"We'll have the brunch tea assortment." Hare handed the waiter back the menus.

That sounded vague.

He patted his chest. "Knowing how to use this won't make you comfortable pulling it on someone."

"I realize that, but if I have to—if I'm in that situation—I'll have more options being armed than not."

He smiled. "You will. After the tasting tonight, I still need you someplace new and safe for a few days. But when I'm done, lessons will be a top priority. Deal?"

She didn't like that he put off her request, but at least he wasn't talking down to her. "Deal. And thank you."

"I wish this thing wasn't so disruptive to your live." He traced his thumb over her knuckles. "I hate it that it came down to extracting you, but I'll do what I can to help you adjust."

Each light touch or gaze helped her feel more normal, and sent pleasant shivers of affection through her. "I guess I brought this on myself."

He shrugged. "Back to questions you have for me. By the way, you sure do dive into the deep stuff first."

"What do you mean?"

"This is a getting-to-know-you chat," he said. "I thought maybe you'd lead with something like *what's your favorite food* or *what kind of music do you like*?"

"Those seem a bit tame, given the situation." A man shot at her yesterday, and she'd cut herself off from her past, to avoid it happening again. Favorites didn't seem important.

He shook his head. "If you abandon *everything* you love, there's nothing to look forward to. Besides, you can tell a lot about a person by how they hold a basic conversation. I'll go first. What's your favorite food?"

"I don't know. I like a lot of things."

"In that case, what's your go-to? If you're tapped for ideas, and nothing else sounds good, or you want that one thing that gives you comfort, what do you turn to?"

"Neapolitan ice-cream sandwiches." The answer tugged loose memories she'd rather not linger on. She shoved aside the sharp sting of the past.

"Why?" He sounded genuinely interested.

Because Alex used to buy them for her whenever he took her to the park. He'd always make her promise not to tell Mom, especially if it ruined Reagan's dinner. The answer was too personal to share. "I like the three flavors all at once, I guess. What about you? Favorite food?"

"Plum cake."

"That's an odd answer."

"I'm an odd person." He winked. "But it's good. Have you ever had it?"

She wasn't even certain what it was. Cake made with plums? Cake with plum frosting? Plums drizzled on the top? "I haven't."

"Then we'll have to change that at some point."

"I'd like that." The exchange was simple, but his offer tugged at an underlying thought she'd been trying to ignore since yesterday. "When does all of this end? Or do I run and hide forever?"

He furrowed his brow, and his smile slipped. "I don't know. I wish I had a better answer than that. You poked a dangerous monster, and I don't know what happens next."

"That makes sense." As much as she wished there was a different way.

"I understand why you made the decision to find this man. That you probably didn't consider the consequences. I don't say that to be rude or dismissive; this isn't the kind of thing you can anticipate unless you've lived it. But you're here now. The only way out is to pick a direction through."

"I get it." And she did. If she was willing to drop this search for Jabberwock and walk away, she might be able to hide. Vanish off the grid and become someone else. It was hard to do in a society as plugged in as this one, but she could find a way.

That meant more running, and if she was going to do that, she wanted answers first. She might not have known what she was getting into when she started looking for Jabberwock, but the big picture was coming into focus. Before she hid, she had to know who this asshole was that he could have people killed on a whim—that had the power to make living life dangerous, no matter where she went.

Chapter Seven

Reagan lingered near the benches against the wall, by the front entrance to the restaurant. Hare had excused himself after brunch and told her he'd join her shortly, before heading toward the restrooms.

Her pulse ticked in her ears. Could anyone else see she was on edge? Each time someone coming or going glanced in her direction, she gave them a tight smile, then went back to trying to survey the entrance and the dining room simultaneously.

Someone pressed against and grabbed her arm, their fingers digging into her skin. The scent of cloves assaulted her, and she blinked away the blur in her vision.

"You're a hard woman to track down." His voice sent ants crawling over her skin. It was the shooter from the church. He stepped closer, and something hard dug into her back, just above her ass. "That's a holstered pistol. I haven't drawn it because I'm not an idiot and there are a lot of witnesses. However, your safety isn't as important as mine. The gun is loaded, and if you scream, if you run, if you try to leave, I *will* shoot you in the back."

She tried to jerk away, but he held her tight. If she screamed, would people come to her aid? Could she run? Where the hell was Hare?

"Do you understand?" he asked.

"Yes." She forced her voice to stay calm, despite the gallop of her heart against her ribs. As long as she was alive, there was a chance of breaking free. She needed to wait for an opportunity. If he was taking her to a car, she could twist away. Grab his gun. Run and hide outside. Find more avenues for exit. Give Hare time to find her.

Her blood rushed so hard in her ears, she wondered how she heard anything else.

"We're going outside." His tone was casual. He slipped an arm around her waist and pointed her toward the door. "Remember—it only takes a second for me to draw and pull the trigger, and I don't miss."

"I understand." She gave a tight smile to the couple passing in the other direction. *Notice us. Do something. Call someone.* Too bad her telepathy was nonexistent.

He guided her toward the parking lot, and she scanned the rows of cars, looking for the best place to dive the moment she had an opening. Instead of stopping near a vehicle, they walked toward an abandoned lot and a patch of weeds, across the street.

If she didn't bolt soon, would she lose her chance? Each step he took her further from the familiar, the dumber it seemed to let him keep leading. She should risk it now and bolt. There was a car a few feet away. Could she reach it and then duck and run behind the nearby building before he hit her? Would he chase her? If his safety was more important than hers, would he risk something like shooting anyone between her and him?

Her stomach dropped into her shoes, as her imagination treated her to images of what it could look like to find out.

A soft grunt reached her ears, before his touch fell away, and he landed on the ground with a *thud*.

Reagan swore her heart stopped.

Someone grabbed her hand and whirled her. She found herself looking at Hare. "We're leaving. *Now*." He bit off the words.

She glanced at her would-be captor, lying on the ground. It took the last of her focus to keep from shaking. She didn't have the will or the desire to argue. She let Hare lead her toward a nearby car—a different one than they arrived in. She slid into the passenger seat and counted the seconds until he was seated and they were driving away from the scene.

Several minutes passed, with him taking a winding maze of turns and glancing in the rearview mirror every few seconds.

"Whose car is this?" She was surprised her vocal chords cooperated enough for her to ask.

"Mine."

"But—"

"Questions later. I need to focus on getting us to safety."

An image surged back into her thoughts, of a body, slumped on the asphalt, limp and unmoving. "Is that guy dead?" There was no blood. Even in her frazzled state, she would have seen blood. No gunshot. No struggle.

Her breakfast surged into her throat, and she swallowed it back.

"Unconscious. Tranquilizer."

"I don't—"

"You have a lot of questions." He glanced at her, sympathy in his eyes, before turning his attention back to the road. "I'd be surprised if you weren't Wayne's Cheshire Cat for as rampant as your curiosity runs. Drive first. Explain later."

"Okay." She wanted to argue but didn't want to distract the closest thing she'd found to a non-threat since this started. The Cheshire Cat reference made no sense. She tried to occupy her mind with figuring out what he meant, but reality shoved the musing aside.

They drove for almost an hour, taking the freeway on ramps, then exiting at the next spot. He followed back streets that led to crowded main roads, then turned down residential streets. She knew the main parts of this city better than most people, but she didn't recognize half the neighborhoods he took them through.

She did recognize the row of brick buildings they parked behind. It was only a few blocks from the spot they'd left a body lying in the parking lot. "Why did we come back here?" It must be all right to speak now. He wasn't looking over his shoulder every few seconds.

"This is where we need to be." He looked at her as if it were obvious. "Besides, whoever was following us isn't there now. But we need to get inside."

He met her in front of the car and guided her

toward a plain, dark-brown door, at the back of the strip. He knocked, and they were let in by a woman who could have stepped straight off the cover of Cosmo. Long neck, hair piled on top of her head without a strand loose, and a peach sundress that showed off her long, thin figure.

Hare smiled. "Thank you, Monique. Give us a moment?"

"Of course. I'll be up front when you're ready." Monique turned away, and a moment later vanished around the corner at the end of the hallway.

Hare turned back to Reagan and grasped her fingertips loosely. Placing a finger under her chin, he pulled her gaze to his. "You have a lot of questions, and I understand why." As he spoke, he searched her face. "I promise I'll explain everything as I'm able. There are things I can't tell you yet, and things you're better off not knowing, but I'll give you the rest. Are you still up for tonight?"

"There are people looking for me."

He squeezed her fingers. "Not there, there aren't. Jabberwock won't disrupt a client meeting for whatever it is he wants with you. It's probably the best place in the city for you to be tonight, especially with me at your side."

She wasn't reassured by his answer. Was she supposed to be? "What about after the wine tasting?"

"I'll make sure you're secure tonight. Do you want to skip the evening? I can find someone to stay with you sooner."

The same logic that warred in her head at brunch rushed back. She was already in deep, and never intended to be. She had no idea what to expect at this gathering, but it was reasonable that it was one of the more secure spots she could be. "If he's hunting *me* now, I want it to stop. I'll attend the event."

"Good." He wrapped an arm around her waist and guided her to the shop. The room they stepped into was a sharp contrast to the nondescript beige carpet and walls they left behind. The boutique was straight out of a movie. Three-fold mirrors stood in different corners of the room, and there were more mannequins than dress racks.

Monique stepped from behind the counter as they approached, and gave Hare a warm smile. "I've set up a dressing room for you. Is there anything the young lady would like to look at first?"

She made it sound as if she knew they were coming. Did Hare call ahead? When did he have time for that?

Monique was watching her, and Reagan said, "No, thank you." At least until she knew what waited for her.

"Let me know if you need any assistance," Monique said.

"We'll be all right," Hare answered before Reagan could. "I'll holler if we need anything."

A spike of frustration, carried on a morning of fear that sat heavy in her gut, jolted Reagan. "I can speak for myself," she said the moment Monique was out of earshot.

"Do you remember the conversation we had this morning—you do what I say, when I say? That starts now. This is you blending in." Hare pointed her toward a door a few feet away.

This was too much. In the last twenty-four hours she'd been shot at, taken at gunpoint, and told more times than she wanted to count. Now she could have answers, but only under some vague, undefined set of circumstances only Hare seemed to know the rules to. She understood his need to not draw attention—she didn't want to stand out—but the rest gnawed at her tentative grip on reality. "I suppose next you're going to tell me part of doing what you say is letting you help me try on… whatever's waiting for me in there."

"If you'd like."

"In other words, I have a choice? This isn't a case of you saying, *I'm footing the bill, you at least owe me a free look?*" She'd find another way to get to Jabberwock if extortion was one of Hare's tactics for getting her to fall in line.

"You don't owe me anything, and you always have a choice." He moved to stand behind her and rested his hands on her hips. His breath was hot on her neck. He was close enough the faint smell of cologne and dry-cleaned clothing penetrated her senses. "Every choice you've made has led you to this point, and you always have a say in what you do next." His voice was quiet, weaving into her thoughts. "However, I *am* arrogant enough to think you'll invite me into the dressing room with you."

"Oh?" She tried to make the question sound aloof and haughty.

"Mhmm." His tone and confidence seared her skin and sent sparks through her veins, gliding on the receding endorphins of having successfully escaped her attacker. He glided his fingers along her waist.

"Because I think you like the idea. I think it sets your nerves on fire. You can almost taste it, like the hint of a memory of sweet on your tongue, and you know it will drive away the tension clawing at your limbs."

Fuck, he was right. She wasn't sure if the lust coiling in her belly was driven more by adrenaline or *him,* but fantasy had skipped several steps ahead. It treated her to images of his fingers gliding over her bare skin, his gaze drinking in her body, as she stripped down in a tiny room with a sales clerk a few feet away on the other side of the door.

"So, my gorgeous ward." He dragged his nose up the side of her neck, and a chill raced down her spine. "Would you like help trying on your new clothes?"

She nodded. "Yes."

Chapter Eight

Hare guided Reagan into the dressing room and closed the door behind them.

She paused to take it all in. She'd expected a closet-sized space with a mirror and a built-in bench. This room was big enough to fit the leather couch and love seat, along with a rack holding three dresses. A pair of heels sat on the floor beside it, and a mirror lined one wall.

"Reagan?" His voice, abrupt compared to the soft music filling the room, jarred her.

She wasn't about to admit to being awed by a changing room, after his insistence she didn't know how to carry herself in certain company. "Just realizing there are no other customers and Monique isn't far away."

"So?" He nudged her further inside. "She's paid not to care. But if it makes you feel better, do your best to bite your tongue, and I'll try just as hard to make you scream." Light teasing lined his words.

"Not happening." It was easier to grasp the playfulness than focus on the rainbow of stresses she couldn't handle. She could see why he said sex was a good temporary escape from tension. Already, desire spilled inside, burning away the tightness in her neck and shoulders.

"Is it at least a little bit of a turn-on?" His lips vibrated against her skin, as he drew them up her neck. "Thinking about someone being a few feet away, out of sight, but not out of hearing range, and most likely enjoying what she hears?"

"I guess you'll have to find out for yourself." Reagan's skin prickled with the need to be touched, and the coil in her belly unfurled, traveling to her fingertips, toes, and sex. She didn't know if she'd ever been this aroused from so little contact. But there was no fun in admitting that.

He moved into view, wearing a smirk. He grasped her fingers and pulled her into the middle of the room. As he looked her over, his gaze left the lingering dust of want everywhere it fell. "You can't try on the dresses if you're in the old clothes. Shirt off."

She liked the simplicity of the command. The fact that she didn't need to question the intent behind it. She stripped off her top and set it aside. Instinct overtook her, and she covered her chest.

"Now you're timid?" Amusement danced in his eyes. "You don't strike me as shy. Jeans and sneakers next."

Wetness pooled between her legs. She stepped from her shoes, pulled off her socks, and then shed her pants. Standing in front of Hare in nothing but her bra and panties, she felt more exposed than at any point in the last couple of days. But the rush of endorphins begged her to keep going, rather than run.

He circled her, looking her over, the appreciative quirk of a smile never fading. This ranked stories above making out in the back seat of a car. Or lying in bed, trying to quietly screw someone, because her roommate slept a door away and had a test in the morning.

This was a rush Reagan could get addicted to.

Hare pointed her toward one of the mirrors. He brushed her ear with his lips. "You're gorgeous." His whisper caressed her cheek. She felt fingers on her back, and a second later, the tension loosened on her bra. He held her gaze in the reflection of the mirror, while he slid her bra straps down her arms. "Don't look away," he said.

Mirror-her stared back at them, lips slightly parted and cheeks flushed, as mirror-Hare glided his hands up her chest to cup her breasts. Reagan moaned and tried to push closer to the barely-there touch across her nipples. Seeing the blonde stranger wearing her face and mimicking her movements added a new level of sensation to the experience.

He slid her panties down her legs next, lifting one foot at time so she could step out, then setting the underwear with the rest of her clothes. "Sit in the chair and spread your legs."

"All right, Mister Bossy."

"*Yes, Sir* will do fine," he said. "And think of it as practice for this evening."

She would roll her eyes at anyone else, for a line like that, but the assurance in his tone glided over her body like a second set of hands. "Except I'm not letting you strip me down in a room full of strangers," she said.

"Not *that* room." He knelt at her feet and looked up at her. "Eyes on the mirror."

Turning back to their reflections blanketed her in the surreal. As the man in the glass kissed up the inside of the woman's thigh, Reagan sank into Hare's mouth sucking along her sensitive skin. She watched mirror-her mimic her squirm, as he drew closer to her core.

When he moved away from the source of her need and worked his way down the other leg, she whimpered and dug her fingers into the arms of the chair. Her hips bucked closer to his touch, but he kept his kisses light and limited to her leg and knee.

Observing the people across from her go through the same things was a new kind of arousing. She found herself thinking of mirror-Hare as a separate person, teasing the other woman. If he decided to grant her release, would Reagan be allowed the same?

Hare moved back up and licked along her pussy. She bit the inside of her cheek, to keep a moan from escaping. He dipped his tongue into her opening, and she squirmed at the needles of pleasure that raced over her.

"Fuck, you taste amazing." He probed her inner walls, drawing her closer to the edge of climax with each thrust of his tongue.

She didn't dare reply. What little control of her vocal chords she had was focused on not crying out. She closed her eyes and tilted her head back, wanting to fall into this moment as herself, and not share it with a reflection.

When he moved his thumb to her clit, she

arched her back, to grind into his touch. He pushed in, drawing tight circles around the swollen button. Her breath came in short gasps. She was vaguely aware of squeaking or maybe groaning, but she wanted to dive into his touch.

Her ass came off the chair, as orgasm crashed through her. She pressed into his attentions and knotted her fingers in his hair, holding him close.

She writhed until her body couldn't take any more, and then she jerked away from him. A shudder racked her, then another, as he kissed the tender flesh before pulling away.

Her throat was raw, and her head swam. It took her a moment to open her eyes. The entire time, he traced lazy circles along her leg.

"I had a feeling I could make you scream." He looked up at her with a sly smile.

Did she? Heat might have flooded her, but she was too flushed to tell the difference. "Point for you." Her word came out as a dry croak. In the back of her mind, the incident from earlier, with the gunman, tried to rush back. The cloud of euphoria filling her thoughts kept it at bay.

He pulled a foil packet from his wallet, and it took her a moment to realize it was a wet-wipe. He cleaned her, his gentle ministrations enough to make her buck, and tossed the tissue away.

"You have dresses to try on." He stood and offered her a hand.

She accepted. "If you insist." There was no fight in her. She was happy to linger in this pocket of bliss.

He pulled a hanger from the rack and held the

black dress in front of her. "This one first."

She stepped into the outfit and tugged it on. The fabric was soft. If she wore anything underneath, there would be lines. The black knit was sleeveless, and followed her curves down to end at her knees.

He stepped behind her and zipped up the back, then handed her the heels. She rose by three inches when she stepped into them.

"What do you think?" he asked.

Mirror-her stared back, judging and appraising. The familiar gaze traveling over her, then moving back to meet her own. "I barely recognize me."

"I know exactly who you are, even if you haven't figured it out yet."

She whirled at the odd words, ready to question him.

"You look stunning." He spoke before she could. He pulled the handkerchief from his jacket pocket, flicked it once to unfurl it, then rolled it up. He reached behind her head, and used the fabric to tie her hair back. "And that's simply elegant. Every eye in the room will be on you tonight."

"That doesn't seem like a good thing." She kept her laugh light.

"It is. You're hiding in plain sight. Except there's nothing plain about you. High cheekbones"—he followed her jaw and up to her brow—"captivating eyes, a cute button nose"—he trailed his finger along her bottom lip, eliciting a sigh—"and full lips I'd love to see around my cock."

She cleared her throat and raised her brows in disbelief.

He grasped her wrist and lowered her hand to trace his erection through his slacks. "Is this more direct?" he asked.

"I wasn't questioning what you meant." She liked the teasing.

He guided her to slide down his zipper. "And you haven't said *no* yet."

"I haven't." She dropped to her knees. That they were doing this in an almost-public place was wicked, but wearing the dress and heels made her feel filthy in the best possible way. She wrapped her hand around his shaft, to free him, and he groaned and leaned into her grip.

As she pumped, she looked up to find him watching her, eyelids half-closed. She drew her tongue along the head of his cock, before taking him in her mouth.

He thrust against her, hitting the back of her throat, and grasped her ponytail. The urgency and control in his grip tingled across her skin, making her wet again. This was the right kind of raunchy and fun.

Salt danced on her tongue as she licked his shaft. He held her head captive, fucking her face, grunts tearing from his throat.

"Your mouth feels so good." His voice had dropped an octave, words coming out in a rumbling growl.

She moaned and widened her eyes, watching him watch her. She paused long enough to say, "I want to taste you."

"Fuck." He gasped the word and increased his pace. He tightened his grip until her scalp stung.

A dull ache spread through her knees, but she

didn't care. She sucked harder. A new kind of desperation welled inside. An intense need to finish him. To please him.

He jerked, and a warm spurt hit the back of her throat. And then another. She whimpered in delight as he came in her mouth. His frantic rhythm slowed, before he stopped.

She licked him clean as she pulled away, smirking in self-satisfaction, he shuddered each time she drew her tongue or lips over his cock.

He helped her stand, pulled the handkerchief from her hair, and wiped a stray drop from her chin. "Absolutely stunning," he said.

This was a different kind of terrifying than being chased by men with guns. This screwed with her thoughts and distracted her and made her want to surrender control, which seemed like a bad idea on normal days. Given her current circumstances, it was outright dangerous.

But—so help her—she was rapidly becoming addicted to the rush that came with the kind of sex Hare offered, and the calm that settled over her after. It helped her push everything into the background for a few minutes.

As long as she remembered it was only a temporary distraction, that she couldn't live there all the time, the momentary lapses from reality were fine.

Chapter Nine

Reagan was grateful that, despite Hare's earlier assurance, the entire room didn't turn to watch them as they entered. In contrast to this morning, she didn't feel underdressed. She had no illusions she'd fit in here on her own, however.

She kept her hand hooked in the crook of Hare's elbow, telling herself she was only doing it for appearances, not because she needed something to hold onto, and not believing the lie.

The conversations around them were quiet enough she heard the tap of her heels on the hardwood and the clink of glasses on tables polished so brightly, they reflected the people sitting at them.

At the far end of the room, a bar spanned the length of the wall. An almost-rainbow of colors lined the top, glasses filled with liquid that ranged from pale beige to the deepest violet. Numbered bottles sat on the shelf behind the bartender, their contents matching the poured wine.

She wanted to pluck one up, down the wine in a single gulp, and move to the next.

Hare handed her a glass and leaned in, his

mouth near her ear. "Possibly the only time you'll ever hear me say this—spit, don't swallow." He pulled back and nodded at a bucket sitting in the middle of a nearby table.

She gave him a tight smile. "Thanks. I know how that bit works." She kept her tone low and sweet, despite the sarcasm she wanted to pour into her response.

"Rules," was all he said.

Right. This wasn't meant to be insulting, but he would assume she knew nothing. "I'm sorry…" Her voice stuck in her throat when they turned to face the room and she saw a familiar face. *Hatter.* He watched them from across the room.

Her stomach churned, and her hand shook. She dug her fingers deeper into Hare's arm and steadied herself.

"What's wrong?" Hare followed her gaze. "Isn't he the reason you're here? Or is reality just sinking in?" He spoke with a conversational cadence, so quietly only she'd hear the words.

That didn't mean what he said made any sense. "I'm here because—"

"One of Jabberwock's top men is meeting with a potential client tonight." Hare nodded at Hatter. "*He's* that top man."

She wanted to retreat. Crawl under a table. Turn on her toe and bolt out the door. Hatter's stare held hers, freezing her feet to the floor.

She wanted to look away, but if she did, Hatter would evaporate again. He was the enemy? "So he knows Jabberwock." She wasn't sure if she wanted to down the drink in her hand or was grateful she hadn't had any yet to sour her insides. She set the glass on a nearby table instead.

Hare made a *tsk* sound with his tongue. "No one *knows* Jabberwock. Not that they could tell you. He works through his representatives. Rumor is, if you realize you've met him, that's when you draw your last breath. He could be anyone. *Fuck.* You could be him, and no one would ever know."

"I really couldn't." Every impulse in Reagan's head screamed *run*. She wasn't sure if it was from Hatter or Hare

Hare shrugged. "Anyway. Hatter is one of his primary representatives."

Oh God. Her legs threatened to give out. She'd screwed him the night Wayne died. Had he been sent to take care of her, too? Why was she still alive? She'd never found pictures. In all her research, it wasn't just Jabberwock whose face was hidden. No one had evidence of any of his people. "You don't know for sure that's true."

"I do." Hare's response came without hesitation. "Because I'm one too."

Reagan's head spun, and her world dropped out beneath her. She was vaguely aware of Hare helping her into a nearby seat and taking the spot next to her. She must have misunderstood what he meant. "You're one what?"

He rested his elbows on his knees and leaned close, leaving only a few inches between them. "One of Jabberwock's representatives."

Jesus-fuck-me-shit. "You lying asshole. You fucked me under false pretenses, you—" There was something more important to worry about. Reagan struggled to draw breath. The walls were closing in around her. "Then he knows where I am." Stating the obvious helped ground her. Gave her a leaping-off point to figure out next steps. The problem was, the leap took her into nothingness. She had no idea what she was supposed to do.

"He has for a while," Hare said.

"Then why am I still alive?"

"Because I'm here." He spoke as if it were the only obvious answer. "I'm on your side. None of his people need to know that, it's between you and me, but as long as you're with me, they won't touch you."

She needed a similar plan to when she was almost abducted after brunch, but to execute it this time. Find a moment when he wasn't looking, and run. Hare let his guard down around her before; it would happen again. Until then, she'd see how much information he gave her, and assume at least half of it was meant to deceive. "What about at the church? The restaurant? Why was someone sent to kill me?"

"I don't have that information. I don't think it was on his command, but we're each privy only to our own orders. This is a really bad place to be discussing this, by the way."

"Because the timing is never right to give me answers." She left the distaste in her words, but did straighten in her seat and paste on a smile for the benefit of any onlookers.

Hare pursed his lips, then pulled her to her feet. Hatter had vanished. Again. Faded into the crowd. She wanted to search every face until she found him. Hare wrapped an arm around her waist, limiting her range of vision, and led her to another room. No one sat on the plush couches or lounges here. She didn't know if she was relieved at the lack of an audience or concerned that it meant no witnesses.

"I was telling you the truth before—that Wayne wasn't working alone. That he wanted to make sure you were safe if anything happened to him. Jabberwock wants you alive—I don't know why—but I'm also here because of Wayne. It took years to entrench myself in this organization and work my way to the top. Please don't blow my cover now."

She shook her head and gave a short laugh. "You're making it hard to believe anything you say. If that's true, why did he approach me the night Wayne died? Was that on orders from Jabberwock as well?"

"You know him." Hare's cool mask slipped, and he raised his brows. His pleasant, neutral expression slipped back in again so quickly, she wondered if she imagined the change.

"He approached me," she repeated. Deceived her. Used her. For all she knew, got off on hunting her. Fuck. Hare could be doing the same thing. Probably was.

"I can't say why." Was that a waver in his voice? No. "We all operate on a need-to-know basis, and I'm not how that applies to him unless it impacts me. It was a mistake to bring you here."

"Then why did you...? Holy shit. You're the one who's supposed to be meeting with the business contact."

"We both are. But I didn't realize you'd met Hatter. That changes everything."

"Does it? You were going to have to tell me anyway, if you were going to connect with this other person. Why am I here in the first place?" And how quickly could she leave? Would he let her walk away now? The man at the restaurant said safety was more important than keeping her alive. She should assume that about everyone.

Hare rested a palm on her cheek and forced her to look at him.

Ice crawled down her skin, raising goosebumps in its wake, and she resisted the desire to jerk away from his touch.

"I told you when we first met I have to be able to trust you as well. This isn't the kind of information I can give to just anyone, if I want to keep my position and stay alive."

It made a kind of sense, but that didn't mean it was true. "Why have you worked so hard to find your way in?" Would she be able to spot another lie if he gave her one?

"Same reason you have." Hare gave her a tired smile. "To find out what happened to Alex. Can we leave now?"

She didn't want to go anywhere with him, but at the same time, running without a plan felt stupid. She nodded and let him lead her back to the valet podium. Questions surged in her head as she waited for the car to be brought around. Which could she ask and get an honest answer?

"Why bring me, if you're going to leave without completing the job?" she asked as they headed away from the country club.

"Hatter can finish things. It was only surveillance. I wanted you to experience the subtlety of the operation and see if you picked up on anything."

The odd statement was enough to pull her out of her spiraling thoughts. "Like what?"

"If I tell you, then you weren't the one who picked up on it."

She clenched her jaw. "That's some cryptic bullshit. Are you tired of giving me answers? Again?"

"If I tell you my perspective, it taints yours. If you see this through your own eyes, it becomes more real. Less filtered."

Unfiltered was the opposite of everything that came out of his mouth. "Where are we going?" she asked.

"I told you earlier, I have other work to do. I'm putting you in a new motel for a few days."

It was too easy. He was going to leave her alone after dropping a bomb like this? She wanted to celebrate. Instead, for appearance's sake, she pouted and slumped in her seat. "Are you sure it's safe?"

He glanced at her. "Someone will keep an eye on you, until I can come back."

"Yay. A new roommate." Did her sarcasm hide the nauseated hope surging inside? And how did this all fall into place so quickly? Where was that point where he stopped watching her for Wayne and Alex, and started carrying out Jabberwock's orders?

"No." Hare smiled. "I'm too selfish for that. He'll watch from a distance."

"Good." She didn't dare say more, for fear of saying too much.

Fifteen minutes later, Hare pulled into the parking lot of a single-story building with a neon *Vacancy* sign flashing near the front office. Inside, he headed toward the check-in desk. "Wait here," he said.

She was tempted to bolt, but if she waited until he left, and made sure she avoided her *guard*, she'd have a lot more of a lead when someone came looking for her.

A few minutes later, Hare handed her an envelope with a number written on it and a key card inside. "I'll make sure your room is secure, though it should be. This is a last-minute decision, so it's not likely to register on someone's radar."

That was good, right? If he didn't plan this, there were no cameras or any way of monitoring her? Assuming he was telling the truth. 'It seemed smarter to err on the side of paranoia at this point.

He accompanied her to her room and dropped the duffel bag that contained the clothes he'd bought her after they left the boutique on the bed. He spent longer than she thought possible examining every inch of the place, from the closet to the shower and including the two inches that separated the bed from the floor.

He stood and smoothed out his suit. "It's clear. Will you be all right here for a couple of days? I'll leave you with money, and the people watching you will be by your side if you go out for food."

"I'll be fine." She gave him a tight smile. With a little luck, he'd interpret it as stress, rather than her mind tripping over the best escape route.

"Good." He kissed her on the cheek. "I'll be back in two days. There's a burner phone in the bag. Call me if you need me."

"Thanks." *You can leave now.* She kept the mental chant from her expression.

After Hare left, she changed quickly. Part of her cringed at the idea of mistreating the expensive dress and shoes. She hesitated, then bundled them as carefully as possible and set them in the duffel bag.

Dressed in clothes more suitable for moving around, she sank to the edge of the mattress. How long did she need to wait before bolting? Where was her guard located, and was there more than one? If she went for a casual stroll around the property, would she be able to tell?

It seemed like a good place to start. While she was out, she could grab something to snack on from the vending machine she saw down the hall.

She opened the door, and her heart dropped into her shoes when she almost smacked face-first into Hatter. "Are you fucking kidding me?" The question escaped before she could stop it.

"Wherever you think you're going, don't." He nudged her back into her room.

She bit off a laugh before it could slip into maniacal. "At the risk of never climbing out of this hell, what else could go wrong?"

"I'd give you a list, but we don't have a lot of time." Hatter hovered near the door, arms crossed, even when she paced to the other side of the room.

"I'm being watched," she said.

"You are. Two men at each exit, and at least

one general on you at all times. Jabberwock ordered me here to check your room, and then leave the rest of his people to nighttime guard duty."

"Well fan-fucking-tastic." She pulled the chair out from the desk and sat. "At least I'm safe." The sarcasm oozing from her voice kept her mind from spiraling into a well of panic and despair.

Chapter Ten

Hatter stared at her for several seconds before speaking. "I'm here in two capacities. As a general, and to tell you I'm your friend on the inside. And thank God you're safe. I've been looking for you for days, terrified I broke my promise to Wayne in under a week."

He had the nerve to force his way into her room, after lying to her in Vegas then following her at the funeral, and act as though *she* was the one who vanished? "Get the fuck out of my room, or I'll mace you."

"Are you hiding the canister in your back pocket? Your bra?" He surveyed the area surrounding her.

"I'll scream."

"If you do that, you won't get answers."

"Answers don't do me any good if they're bullshit." She was tired of being threatened. At least he was in her face about it, rather than shooting her in the back. What did she need to say, to get him to leave? "Besides, I have answers, and I was promised I wouldn't have an in-room babysitter."

"I told you I'm only here long enough to make sure you're settled." As he spoke, he made his way around the room, lifting the receiver on the phone. Unscrewing the mouthpiece. Checking the lamps—shades and bulbs. Looking under the bed.

"Right. The armed contingent who's here to keep me safe, even though it makes it sound like I'm a prisoner." She'd already been sucked into one mind-fuck, she didn't have the sanity for a second.

Hatter pinched the bridge of his nose and slid to the floor, back against the door. "Wayne didn't tell you."

"He told me a lot of things." She didn't think for a second that just because Hatter had his back to her, he wasn't on his guard. Despite not seeing him in action, she had no reason to suspect he wasn't as well trained as Hare. "He stopped short of advising me to wear a tinfoil hat, but he did make me carry a purse lined with copper mesh."

"That means in Las Vegas you thought I was... *Shit.*"

"No. I thought you were a smooth-talking, sexy-as-fuck businessman, who liked to slum it a little. Not a hired henchman. I'm starting to think you're a shit, though."

"Can we start over?" he asked.

She'd like that. Not in the way or for the reasons he probably meant, but more like going back to when Wayne told her to be on her guard, and instead of ignoring him, she ran as fast as possible in the other direction. "Sure. I apologize for interrupting your script."

He narrowed his eyes. "That night in Vegas,

when you refused to come home, Wayne asked me to keep an eye on you."

"Did he tell you to fuck me, too? Because that doesn't sound like the guy I knew."

"No, Alice—"

"Don't call me that." She barked out the words. "How did this supposed conversation go? He told you I had a thing for intelligent, witty men, and you figured that was your way in?"

"I thought you knew who I was. I wasn't going to walk up to you and say *Wayne sent me*, if Jabberwock's men—besides me—were watching you, but Wayne assured me he would tell you to look for me. You were pretty straightforward about your interests."

"I thought it was a random hook-up." She was seconds away from shouting. Not because she thought it would do her any good, but she needed an outlet for her frustration. "Do you try to prove yourself next? Tell me you know things no one else possibly could? That you knew and adored my brother, and you want to get revenge and help me in the process? Because I've already heard a version of that story, and wherever you people are getting your lines, you need to compare notes better so I don't hear the same crap twice."

"Are you done?" His tone was flat.

"For now."

"Fantastic. Forgive me while I pick this apart. What happened to your brother?"

That nagging hesitation was back, making her doubt her self-assurance. "You need to read the script more closely next time. Hare knew."

"Wayne never told me anything about a brother. He suspected your enthusiasm for the subject matter was more than idle curiosity, that you were too driven for it to be otherwise, but he said you never gave him a story beyond *because I want to know, that's why.*"

All this information—figuring out where to look and what to hear and who to trust—was going to give her vertigo. "Then how did Hare know Alex…"

"Was killed by Jabberwock?" Hatter finished for her. "Don't blame me if I'm wrong, but if that's what you were going to ask, my guess would be it's because that's who Hare works for."

"So do you."

"Guilty as charged, or those men outside wouldn't have let me in. Look, Alice—what do I need to prove to you I'm the one telling the truth?"

She clenched her jaw. "You could start by calling me by my name."

"Sorry. Habit. That's what Wayne always called you, so it's what's stuck in my head."

Wayne *did* always call her that. Hare never had. More confusion sank in.

Hatter stood and crossed the room. He extended his hand. "My name's Blake Allen. It's nice to meet you, Reagan."

"Sure it is." She shook his hand, distrust and chaos raging in her head. "Let's say I pick your version of the story over Hare's. Why are you telling me any of this? Are you hoping to convince me to run?"

"God, no. A few days ago, that was the plan.

Now, you're in a lot deeper than you should be. It's going to take time to figure out how to extract you."

"Extract me? Who are you? You work for Jabberwock, but your friends with Wayne, but you have some miracle master plan to take me away from this fucked-up reality. Oh, God, I'm imagining you, aren't I? There was something in the wine."

Blake stared at her, lips pursed.

"Are you going to answer my questions?" she asked.

"Sure. Assuming you meant all of them. I'm Blake Allen—we covered that. You're not imagining me. And I work for people who want Jabberwock gone. As you can imagine, he doesn't know that, and I'd like to keep it that way. And no, I'm not a figment of your imagination. Are we on the same page?"

"If I say *yes*, what am I supposed to do until this mystical extraction happens? Play along with Hare? Pretend this is all fine?"

Hatter—Blake—nodded. "You looked like you were doing all right at the country club."

"Because I didn't know who Hare was until I saw you. Now I don't know who either of you is."

He crouched, to look her in the eye. "I don't have a lot of answers either. But I'll tell you everything I know. I have to leave now, but my shift to keep an eye on you starts tomorrow, and I'll answer any questions I can when I return."

"Convenient. So just like that, you pop in here, feed me a bunch of crap, and then leave." This was too much. She couldn't think with the contradictory and convenient information he and Hare gave her.

He handed her a business card. "Memorize this, then destroy the card. Call me from a landline if you need me. One that's not in this motel. And don't run once I'm gone. I won't stop you, but the men watching your room will."

"Why?" She didn't understand that. If she wasn't a prisoner, why put so much effort into keeping her here?

"Because someone is looking for you, and they know how to spot an unwelcome tail. If you give us the slip, we can't guarantee whoever else is out there won't take you out in an instant."

Reagan didn't have a response for that. Not having seen evidence that supported his claim. "All right. I'll stay put."

She showed him to the door, and latched every possible lock after he was gone. She slid a chair under the door handle, then collapsed on the bed, fully clothed. She stared at the ceiling, hoping it would give her answers.

Blake's story rang true. It was solid, even if it was a repeat of one she'd already heard. But if he was honest with her, her instinct for who was right and wrong was so out of whack, she'd let Hare lead her around for the last several days and never questioned it, because he knew some key snippets of information about her relationship with Alex.

Which meant she was a shitty judge of character, no matter whom she believed. Unless they were both lying. That would make more sense. Not that she understood what the point would be. She was a lowly Master's student from Nowhere-ville, whose only connection to something exciting was that her brother was killed by a mob boss.

She didn't have a fascinating life of her own. Why would they put her through any of this? If she could figure out motivation, it would give her a direction to look. Without it, she only had a name. The one name she'd had all along, that hadn't gotten her anywhere.

But that wasn't true. She had Blake's name now. She hoped. And though she didn't have Hare's real name, everyone they encountered so far called him *Hare*. That was more than she'd ever had before.

Next thing she needed was a computer. If it was true that the motel was being watched, would they follow her when she left? She'd need to eat in the morning, and Blake said he'd be back then. It seemed like an appropriate time to find out what happened if she wandered out in public.

If she was going to do this, she needed sleep. Not the half-assed stuff she'd had for the past week, but real, solid sleep.

She stripped out of her clothes, climbed under the covers, and willed herself to pass out.

She stared at the clock instead, watching it tick past midnight, then toward morning. She dozed off sometime around five. When she pried her eyes open, the clock read 8:14. Her neck felt like someone had shoved a rod down her back, then bent it. New plan—down a bottle of ibuprofen from the motel drugstore first, then get breakfast and find out how close an eye they kept on her.

A shower helped ease some of the aches but didn't chase away the exhaustion. Fortunately, a thrum of tension ran through her, keeping her jittery regardless of the tiredness. If she could grab some coffee, the bigger the better, she might not have to sleep again for a couple of days.

She dressed in the one casual outfit she had—she'd need to find the laundry in this place—grabbed her purse and the stack of cash Hare gave her, and headed out. As she stepped outside, she surveyed the parking lot. There were a couple of cars with a person each. Most of the vehicles were empty. She didn't see anyone else. Were these the people watching her? Did she get a lapse in security?

There was a diner across the street. She'd use that as a starting point to decipher if Hatter and Hare were telling the truth about security.

She hadn't made it halfway across the parking lot, when Blake fell into step beside her.

"I told you I'd be here." He matched her pace.

She glanced sideways, forcing herself not to stare. Unlike the last two times she saw him, he wasn't in a suit today. His jeans were faded and his button-down shirt sleeves rolled up, and a night's worth of scruff decorated his jaw. Apparently he was sexy, no matter what.

Great. She spent the last couple of days literally fucking around with a man who might or might not be her captor, and now she was drooling over the second guy who possibly fit the same description. She needed to get her priorities straight.

"I slept with him." She wasn't sure why she said it. Maybe because it felt good to be the one who knew something for a change. "Hare, I mean." Or maybe she just wanted the satisfaction of seeing Hatter flinch, which he did.

"None of my business." His tone was cool.

She jammed her hands in her pockets. "Are you here to make a note of everything I say and report to the guy up top?"

He nodded across the street. "That young lady leaning against the drugstore next to the diner? Looks like she's probably in her late teens—she may be, for all I know. Dark hair and glasses?"

"I see her."

"That's Ten."

"As in, Ten of Hearts?" Reagan couldn't keep the disbelief from her voice. Jabberwock sure took this shit seriously.

They reached their destination, and Hatter held the door open for Reagan. "Ten of Diamonds. Only the best for you."

"Wouldn't the King of Diamonds be the best? Or the Ace?" The sign near the front said *Seat Yourself. We'll be with you shortly*, so Reagan picked a booth at the back of the room that had a clear view of the door. Hatter slid in next to her, rather than taking the seat across the table. She wanted to be dismayed, but there was something reassuring about having him between her and whatever waited outside. "I loathe couples who do this," she said.

"Good thing we're not a couple. And there's no royalty in Jabberwock's court, besides himself. Anyway, Ten is the closest thing we have to company. As long as you don't say anything she can hear, our conversation is between us."

"Am I a prisoner?" Reagan asked.

Hatter knitted his brows and frowned. "No. Definitely not. I told you last night, we're here to keep someone from trying to either kill or kidnap you."

A waitress stopped at their table. "Can I get you two anything to drink? Do you need a minute to decide?"

"Coffee, please." Reagan's request overlapped and blended with Hatter's.

He smiled. "A lot of it. Make sure you keep an eye on our cups."

"You got it, hon." The girl turned toward the kitchen.

Reagan felt like a fairytale princess—stuck in her tower, waiting for someone to come along and rescue her. She'd go stir crazy if she let this continue.

Last night, Blake said he'd answer any question she had. Time to put that to the test. Hare was good at redirecting half her inquiries. Would Hatter be the same?

"You said you were here on official business, as a general. This seems like a tame detail, for someone so important. What kind of strings did you pull, to land here?" she asked.

"None." He grabbed his phone and swiped the screen as he spoke. "I'm on for twelve hours, and when I leave, Dormouse takes my place. Orders straight from the top."

For her? What made her so important? "Hare says no one has met the guy at the top. Not anyone who realizes it, anyway."

"That's true."

"How do you know it came from *him*, if you've never met him? Maybe Hare sent it. Or this Dormouse. Or Ten."

He slid his phone to her. There was an email on the screen. "We use an app that encrypts messages. His orders come through it, and nothing else. A note here is as good as law in the organization."

"How do you even get a job like this?" Reagan wanted to know so much.

He pocketed his phone. "You know someone who knows someone, and you work your way up from there. I don't understand why Wayne was so worried about you. Or rather, I do on a personal level, but you're getting treatment from Jabberwock that no one does. I should ask how *you* found a gig like this."

"You really shouldn't; I have no idea." If she did, maybe she could find a way out of all of it.

Chapter Eleven

The moment Reagan returned to her room, she picked up the room phone and dialed 911.

Someone picked up on the third ring. "Nine-one-one, what's your emergency?"

"I'm, uh…" What was she supposed to say? Something pretty close to the truth. "I'm being held against my will in a motel room."

"All right Miss, I understand. Are you safe right now?"

"Yes. I'm not allowed to leave, though. There's no one in the room with me, but they're watching me."

"I see." Was that disbelief in her voice or calm professionalism? "If you give me your address and room number, I'll dispatch someone immediately."

Reagan relayed her location. "Tell them to be careful. Maybe send more than one person?"

"Yes, Miss. I understand."

The line went dead. Reagan stared at it. That went too smoothly, and at the same time, it didn't feel like enough of a conversation.

Someone hammered on the door, and her heart leaped into her throat. The police weren't here already. Wrong room? She clenched her hands into fists, to keep them from shaking as she went to answer.

She looked through the peephole and saw Hatter. Ambivalence spilled inside, and she opened the door. He was scowling as he held up his phone and replayed the conversation she'd just had.

"Don't do it again," he said.

"How—?"

"Don't. I won't always be the one to intercept, and regardless of what he wants you for, I'm sure there are limits. While we're on the topic—when we go out to eat, don't try anything like slipping someone a note or sneaking out the bathroom window. We have shoot-to-kill orders if we're concerned about someone approaching you. The directive is fairly open ended. I promise I'm working on a way to get you out. You need to play along until then."

She had no words for that, so she let the door slam shut in his face. "*Fuuuuuuuuck,*" she screamed at the wall.

The next meals were a repeat of breakfast. Reagan tried to mix up the monotony by leaving through one of the other exits. Hatter always fell into step beside her within a few minutes of her walking outside. For breakfast the next morning, she tried grabbing an oversized set of clothes from the gift shop and using them and baseball cap to hide who she was as she left.

He was still there. "Same place for

breakfast?" he asked, strolling next to her.

"Do have a choice?" She was irritated by the restrictions on her activities, but she could think of far worse ways to spend the time. Hatter was good company. She didn't believe for a second that he was trying to help her, but at least the playing pretend-friends was a distraction.

"I'm supposed to follow you wherever you go. We can hop a bus and ride downtown if you'd like. Or there's a Mexican place a few blocks away that's open twenty-four seven."

She knew the place he was talking about. Her stomach couldn't handle peppers this time of the morning. "McDonalds?"

"Sure." His scrunched-up expression defied his casual acceptance.

Fifteen minutes later, they sat in a booth at the back of the restaurant, him with coffee, and her with pancakes and the largest, sweetest caramel mocha they offered.

"You could have gotten those at the diner," he pointed out.

"Not the drink. Besides, I wanted a change of scenery." And to figure out how far her leash stretched. "Do you really have to go anywhere I say?"

"In the city. The goal is to keep whoever shot at you from doing it again. Don't push your luck. Dormouse isn't as forgiving as I am."

She was willing to test that limit, too. She kept the retort to herself, and dug into her breakfast.

"Question for you." Blake held his cup but didn't take a drink. "Why were you with Hare at the wine tasting?"

She'd been trying to figure that out herself. "Because I asked nicely and batted my eyelashes?"

"Really." His voice was flat. "We're supposed to be keeping out of trouble, and he got the okay to drag you into an affair where we had limited ability for crowd control, *and* were studying a perspective contact. How does that work?"

"I wish I knew. He told me he wanted me to watch for something, but refused to say what. It was all hyper-cryptic." The longer she thought about it, the less it made sense.

"Hmm."

They didn't say anything else as she finished her food. She pushed her tray away and grabbed her coffee, but she wasn't ready to go back to her room yet. "You got a question, can I have one in return?"

"Depends on what the question is. You won't know until you ask."

She'd take that. "Who do you work for?"

"Jabberwock."

Not the answer she hoped for. When Blake mentioned extraction, he implied it was someone else. "How do you know Wayne?"

"That's two questions."

"Fine." She puffed a breath up, to blow her bangs out of her face. "Keep a tally and ask me in return."

His shoulders seemed to relax, and he leaned back in his seat. "Same way you do. I found him in a conspiracy theory forum, and after several months of talking, we decided we trusted each other enough to meet."

"Except you neglected to tell him who you work for."

Blake shrugged. "We keep an eye on anyone who's digging into the guy up top. Ninety-nine percent of the time, they don't know enough for it to matter. They fuel the rumors, rather than threatening them."

"So what did Wayne do differently that cost him?"

He scrubbed his face, and when he finished didn't meet her gaze. "I wasn't involved in that. Wayne was a good guy. I liked him."

If the orders come down from the top to kill me, will you step in? She swallowed the question, unsure she could handle any answer beyond a resolute *Of course*, and certain she hadn't earned that kind of emphatic response.

"I get another question." Blake's tone shifted to something too bright.

"Okay."

"Your thesis, all the things you've learned about digital security, was it all because of what happened to your brother?"

The reminder of Alex weighed on the memories of Wayne, and a fist clenched around her heart, until she almost gasped at the pain.

"I'm sorry." Blake shook his head and leaned in to rest his elbows on the table. "I shouldn't have mentioned him."

"It's okay." She could talk about school without dwelling on Alex. She counted to ten, and stashed the past away as best she could. "I can't say for certain, since I picked my major after... *it* happened. But I was heading in this direction anyway. The events gave me a little extra motivation, is all."

"I get that." He worked his jaw up and down, then shook his head.

She wanted to pry for more, but had a feeling he wouldn't give her an answer anyway. "How about you? Did you always know you wanted to be a super-secret, double-employed general for, well, you know?" She swallowed the phrase *crime syndicate.* The restaurant was almost empty, but that didn't mean she wanted to draw attention from the smatter of people who might overhear them.

His chuckle was dry. He fiddled with the label of his cup, shredding tiny pieces of the paper where they met Styrofoam. "When I was little, I wanted to be a super hero. Spiderman, specifically. Normal guy, stuck in an unfortunate situation, who doesn't seize what he's got until he loses someone who matters."

"How close are you to living the dream?" She couldn't ignore the hint of sadness in his reply.

"I think I'd have to be the good guy for any of the rest to matter."

"Aren't you?"

He shook his head. "Once upon a time, I thought so. Now, I'm pretty sure the answer is *no.*"

"Why?"

"That's enough." He stood and tossed his cup in the trash. "I should get you back to your room."

You mean my cell. She kept the response to herself. The venom for her situation was still there, but she couldn't bring herself to direct it at Blake.

When she returned to her room, a padded envelope sat in the middle of her bed, with her name in a neat script on the front.

She tore the flap open. When she upended the envelope, a cell phone dropped to the bed, and a card fluttered out after.

The phone was identical to the one Hare took from her, minus the smears on the glass and scratches on the plastic. She reached for the power button out of instinct, and then paused and read the note with it instead.

I cloned the data on your phone. This one doesn't have a SIM card. You can't use it to make calls, and it can't be traced back to you, but I thought you might want your data back. I promise I didn't go through any of it.

I'm sorry to be away so long. We'll talk soon.
Hare

She didn't know what to make of the gesture, or even if the note was genuine, but she needed to do *something*. She powered on the device, and a moment later was sifting through the documents and photos on it.

Some of her notes about her thesis were there. Not all of them, but the ones she'd worked on most recently. Reading material for tonight. There had to be something to point her toward Jabberwock that she'd missed. She couldn't fathom any other reason he'd go to so much trouble to remove her from her life and imprison her in limbo.

She flipped to the pictures next. There were some from Las Vegas, a bunch from Mindy's last birthday party, and *oh*... Her throat tightened up when she landed on one of Alex. It wasn't one she took. Right before he vanished—*died*—he sent her a batch of them.

She was never able to look through the complete set before. It hurt too much to see him smiling at the camera, knowing she wouldn't see his face in person again.

Today she kept swiping the screen, even as grief forced tears to her eyes and made her sniffle every few seconds. She was having trouble seeing, when a blur of pale caught her attention. Dragging the back of her hand across her cheeks, she forced herself to focus and backtracked to the image.

Hare. Clear as day. Blond hair pulled back, clothing immaculate, and standing next to Alex, their arms draped over each other's shoulders.

"What the fuck?" She flipped faster through the images, until she found several more of the two of them together.

What did it mean? Hare said he knew her brother, and Blake was right—she never told Wayne about him.

When Hare said, *We'll talk soon*, what did that mean? Because God damn it, if Reagan didn't have more questions than ever.

She needed to do something, or she would pace a rut in the carpet. Inspiration struck, and she went to the closet, where she'd hung the dressier clothes Hare bought her. She grabbed the corset and skirt from the back of the short row. When he bought her the outfit, she had no idea what she was supposed to do with it. The blue top was trimmed with gold and had a white, satin panel running down the middle of the front. The skirt was the same blue as the top, and ended halfway down her thighs.

It was almost cosplay ludicrous and perfect for what she wanted to do tonight. She'd stand out in a crowd, even if she went to a place where people were in flamboyant outfits. So when she found her chance to duck into the restroom, change into the shirt and shorts folded into her purse, and hopefully pawn her clothes off on someone else, she could vanish.

She dressed, pulled her hair into a twist on the back of her head, and headed toward the exit. She made a quick stop at the front desk, wearing her brightest smile for the clerk. "Excuse me." She poured sugar into her voice. "I need a cab. Could you call someone for me?"

"Sure." He reached for the phone, gaze never leaving her chest.

"Thank you," she called as she turned away. "I'll be out front."

She stepped into the warm evening and moved away from the entrance to wait, as she counted. She was on forty-Mississippi, when a woman stepped up by her side.

"You're not really dressed for loitering," the woman said.

Reagan looked her over. She wore a silk blouse and pressed slacks and definitely didn't look like she was blending. "Are you Eight? Or Red Queen?"

"I'm Dormouse. There is no other royalty in *his* court."

Almost exactly what Hatter said. "*Dormouse.*

Doesn't really roll off the tongue like *Hatter* or *Hare*."

Dormouse raised her brows. "Tell me, which of the two rolls off your tongue more easily?"

Reagan should be offended by the snark, but it was nice to talk to someone who wasn't pretending they cared about her. "Haven't decided yet. The way I understand it, if you're Hatter's equal, do you follow me wherever I go?" It felt odd to call him by that name. When did he become *Blake* to her?

"That's the decree."

"I'm going dancing."

"No crowded places."

Reagan scoffed. "The *street* is a crowded place the right time of day. I want to go dancing. Desk guy called me a cab—which I assume you already know. Go with me or stay here." Or find some new way to physically restrain Reagan. *Please don't let it come to that.*

"I pick the club," Dormouse said.

Not the answer Reagan expected, and far better than she hoped for. "Fine."

Reagan wasn't interested in making conversation with Dormouse during the ride. The sarcasm might be fun, but she had too much to sift through and determine truth-or-not. She didn't need to add another flavor to the mixture.

The building they pulled up in front of was brick, in the middle of a block of shops with bars over windows sporting *For Lease* signs. "Do you people do anything in places that aren't surrounded by squatters?"

"If you haven't figured it out yet, a lot of what

we do is about appearances." Dormouse looked Reagan over, then reached past her, to push the cab door open. "Building straight ahead, with the tattered awning."

"Swell." Reagan stepped onto the sidewalk and waited for her current *friend* to lead the way. Her heart hammered so hard, she swore everyone could hear it. That now-familiar rush of endorphins pulsed in her veins, beating in time to the mantra in her head. *Freedom. Soon. Finally.*

Dormouse bypassed the glass door and walked through a metal one to the side. As it swung shut behind them, the street noise from outside vanished, and the faint sound of music reached Reagan's ears.

Dim lights lined wooden steps, the shadows hinting at deep scratches and scuffs. Reagan and Dormouse walked downstairs, twisting around three corners before reaching the landing. The music had grown to a beat that thumped through Reagan's feet.

A neon sign hung over a second door, and two doormen guarded it. Dormouse nodded to them, and they moved aside, so the women could enter.

"You're not my problem for the evening," Dormouse whispered in Reagan's ear.

Reagan looked up to see Hare a few feet away, casual smile in place. He extended his arm. "You look stunning, my dear."

Reagan should have thought this plan through a little better. She didn't know how she was going to slip out of this place, with him by her side and the fact they were at least a story underground.

Her plan slipped to her gut, churning with

sick frustration. She'd had a chance, and it was gone. Hare kept his gun in a holster under his jacket. Could she get to it before him? Would she dare use it?

If she turned and ran, would everyone be shocked long enough for her to make it to the street? Would she be tackled before she reached the stairs? Shot in the back when she cleared the door?

She pulled out her brightest grin and hooked her hand around Hare's elbow. Maybe she could lure him someplace private and get the drop on him. And until then, while she was here, she could try to get answers about how he knew Alex.

Chapter Twelve

The first thing Reagan noticed when Hare led her through a flimsy curtain was how the neon lights clashed with the pastel upholstery. It took less than a second for her attention to be drawn to the patrons. People in various states of undress lounged on sofas. Some wore what looked like virtual reality goggles, while others seemed to be observing the scene.

A few feet away, a woman reclined in her seat, wearing nothing but the VR glasses. One leg was slung over the arm of her chair, and *eat me* was written on her stomach. Her head was tilted back, her legs slightly parted, and her nipples were swollen and pink, blending into tan skin. A second woman knelt between her legs. Reagan wasn't at the right angle to see what she was doing, but their moans, loud enough to overlap the dance beat in the room, filled in the details.

Reagan wanted to look away, but the moment held her captivated. Thoughts of fleeing lingered in the back of her mind, but they were overshadowed by the rush of heat flowing through her veins. She squeezed her legs together, but it didn't relieve the throb between. The public display both embarrassed and fascinated her.

"*Eat me*. Appropriate." Hare's voice in her ear mingled with her awe, rather than disrupting it.

She forced herself to stop staring, but focusing on his pale blue stare was its own distraction, and the other pockets of guests were at least as lewd. She turned her gaze to her feet instead.

"Don't do that." Hare placed a finger under her chin and raised her head so she'd look back at the two women. "Not if you like what you see."

As she watched, her body reacted to every touch and groan. The phantom graze of fingers on nipples. The velvety swipe of a tongue along her pussy. The arch of her back with pleasure. "I'm not—"

"A prude. I know that." His voice was heavy, and free of accusation. "If they didn't want to be seen, they wouldn't be in a place like this. They probably enjoy being the show as much as you enjoy observing them." He moved behind her and trailed his fingers along the back of her neck. He tugged at the zipper of her corset to tighten the fabric around her breasts, but not enough to undo anything. "Would you like to become one of the displays? You've drawn some attention."

Her heart slammed into her ribs, and the pulse from her belly to her sex increased. Everywhere he touched tugged a cord that raced to her core, making her want more. This was the same rush she got before. The surge of lust that buried her fear and ate at her adrenaline until it became euphoria.

It would be easy to drown in those sensations.

She could push aside the last several days and let this go where it would. Would she let him strip off her top? Expose her like that? The hopeful gazes watching her from the shadows made the idea both terrifying and arousing.

And if she let Hare distract her like this every time they spoke, she'd never get anywhere. She forced resolution through her veins and turned to face him, taking her attention off the seductive room. "No. I'd like to talk."

"That's fine. There's a seat over there." He nodded in the direction of the two women behind her.

She refused to follow his line of sight. "Someplace quiet. If you're working, I'll wait. In an office maybe? Even a dressing room." Which could be what she needed, in order to slip away.

He waved, and a moment later, Dormouse joined them.

"I have to cut out for a little while. Are you good here?" Hare asked.

"Better than parked outside that fucking motel," Dormouse said.

Hare smiled and grasped Reagan's hand. "I was hoping you'd feel that way." He led Reagan to the other side of the room, through another set of flimsy curtains, and down a long hallway. As they walked further from the club, the decor shifted from plush pastels and stucco walls to brick and concrete. There was no single point where it changed. It was more like someone tried to smear the surroundings but didn't manage to do it uniformly.

He led her into a room at the end of the hall, and the world vanished behind them when the door closed. "Have a seat."

She dropped onto an overstuffed easy chair. Simply being in here was enough to bring her pulse down and smooth her fractured thoughts. The carpet was beige, and the kind of thick that feet sank into. The walls were a shade paler, and the furniture a shade darker. But rather than looking like it was off a showroom floor, the space felt used and lived in. Comfortable.

He sat across from her, which was a relief. "I hope you had a chance to catch up with Hatter."

"I did." She kept the response intentionally short, trying to limit it to information Hare already hadm. Letting too much out felt like giving him leverage, and since she didn't have any idea what he wanted—what Jabberwock wanted—everything she knew had to be held close.

"How'd that go?"

"We caught up." If she was lucky, the vague answers would frustrate him as much as they did her.

His smile disrupted that hope. "Good. Then you probably figured it out by now."

Her stomach clenched. She had suspicions about a lot of things but wouldn't tip her hand. "What's that?"

"That one of us always lies and one of us always tells the truth."

"Nice." Her sarcasm dripped from the word. That was what she needed—more cryptic Alice-in-Wonderland shit. "Also, ridiculous. I mean the entire concept, by the way."

"Good point. It's from a story about a girl who gets bored with her own life and lands in an alternate world, where so many things are familiar but nothing is quite what she expects." He studied her for a moment. "Is it really that ridiculous?"

She didn't appreciate the parallel drawn to her life, but she couldn't argue it. "I mean the *one of us lies* concept, which I don't even know if that originated with Alice. Let's start with, the two doors take turns sharing the riddle. If one of them is lying, then the riddle becomes gibberish. There's no need for fancy questions; they already broke their own rules."

"So what you're saying is you don't trust either one of us."

That wasn't her point, but it was true. "I don't."

"Smart. Like your logicked out interpretation of the riddle, we both have our lies and our truths, but one of us is being more honest with you than the other. Did you get the phone?" he asked.

The sharp change in subjects jarred her, but it was also a reminder she had questions about the photos. "I did…" She pulled it from her purse. "Do you know what was on it?"

"I was sincere when I said I didn't look, but I have a few guesses. That's why I figured you'd want it back."

Would he give her a straight answer about Alex? Because that was one thing she wanted to know rather than assuming. "I'd like to hear why."

"Besides the fact it's your phone, and most people store everything on those devices…" He sighed and tugged his ponytail as his gaze flitted around the room. *Odd.* He finally focused on her again. "Right before he died, he sent you a folder of photos. I screened them, to make sure there wasn't anything damning in them. I assume you still have them, given how driven you are for answers."

"So you realize you're in several of them?"

Hare nodded. "Alex was one of us. He was White Rabbit."

Fuck. Reagan's head exploded with questions and shattered expectations. She thought maybe Alex had borrowed money from the wrong people or gotten stuck in the middle of a deal he couldn't get out of. One of those was more likely than this out-of-nowhere story. "My brother wasn't a ranking officer for an underground crime syndicate."

"He was. I'm in those pictures because we were close. I loved Alex dearly as a friend, and I trusted him with my life."

"If he'd gotten the same from you, would he still be alive?" She couldn't keep the bitterness from her voice. The revelation overwhelmed her. She wasn't sure she could believe it, but if it was true, she was further than ever from understanding the situation.

"There are some things that can't be stopped. Even those of us at the top have to follow the rules."

Reagan shook her head. The stress of the past week threatened to break her. Her skull felt like it was miles from her body, severing, looking down, not understanding how immensely fucked up the world around her had become. "He wasn't White Rabbit. He couldn't have been."

Hare's eyes shone with sympathy and hurt. "Is it harder to believe that than to think he was a low-end thug, picking up the crumbs to survive?" Disdain leaked into his words.

"Yes." She didn't feel as much conviction as she should.

"Why?"

It was obvious, wasn't it? Perhaps not from Hare's twisted world-view. She struggled for the words to defend her belief. "Because at the bottom, he did what he needed to, in order to survive. At the top…" This was coming out wrong.

"He enjoyed it? He paid for your college. He made sure you didn't go without. He found what he was good at, did what was needed to rise in the ranks, and excelled."

Alex didn't pay for her college, she was there on scholarship, and her spending money came from work. Did Hare know that and was trying to trip her up, or was this a secret of Alex's?

"He couldn't have been that good; it got him killed." Why did learning this hurt so much? Her throat was raw, and her hand clenched into an involuntary fist. Alex was good and kind, and— sure—he had his rough patches, but he was her brother.

Hare frowned. "Believe what you want. I can't change that."

"But you can. It would help if you told me a consistent story. For instance, why you never mentioned any of this before. Why you keep turning me away from answers to most of the questions I ask. At least add some continuity to your lies. Then I might be suckered in a little longer."

He held up a finger. "I told you up front I

didn't know if I could trust you. I still don't. I twisted some things, to find out what you knew. Honestly, I expected it to be a little more, but I've tried not to deceive you. *Someone* is working this organization from the inside; it's just not me. *Someone* is hunting you. It's not us, though. *I* swore to Alex I'd keep you safe."

"Why did you tell me this had to do with Wayne?" She didn't know where one lie ended and the next began. If she tugged the right thread, would it all unravel?

"Would you have believed me if I told you otherwise? You had the pictures. I thought you'd recognize me at the funeral. When you didn't, I had to figure out where to go next. You refused to talk to me. When you finally did, you had an entire alternate reality already created that I had to break through. It's not easy to chip away at the foundations of someone's beliefs."

There were so many holes in his explanation, Reagan didn't know where to start. Part of what he said rang true. For the first time since she met him, she felt like he wasn't hiding everything.

Only most things.

"Hatter and Dormouse told me their orders come from the top. They're not following me around, pretending to be my bestest friends, because of something *you* promised," she said.

Hare winced. "Do you know who wants to kill you?"

"No."

"Neither do we. We also can't determine why you weren't taken out at the same time as Wayne."

Because I was with Hatter. How did she know that was true? "Jabberwock had Wayne killed."

Hare shrugged. "We can hash this out all night, and it's still going to take time for you to absorb it."

Another brush-off. So much for getting the whole truth. "What do you suggest I do? I'm not going to sit in that fucking motel room for the rest of my life."

"Stay with me tonight."

That held its own set of problems. "So we can go another round of *fucking masks the stress*?"

"If you'd like. But I don't think that's a good idea. It's a change of scenery and a chance to regroup and see if I can plead to have your circumstances changed."

"*No*. I'm sick of someone I've never met determining my fate because… I don't even know why. If it was to keep me out of danger, I wouldn't be holed up less than twenty miles from home."

"And if I was told to stick you on a plane to the Dominican Republic, to start a new life, would you go without arguing?"

She crossed her arms and pouted as she sank lower in her chair. It was a childish reaction, but she was coming up short on rational ones. "No."

"If you leave with me tonight, I can take some of the pressure off for a few days. Give you a little more freedom and throw the dogs off your scent until we have a longer-term solution."

This was too easy. "What do I have to do?"

"Take off your dress."

She raised her brows. "We already had that part of the conversation."

"I'll turn around, if you'd like to pick now to be modest. I'll have one of the girls bring you something else to wear. She'll put on your clothes and leave with Dormouse, and you'll exit through the rear door with me, while she'll hang out in your motel room for a few days, pretending to be you."

It was a good plan. Enough like hers she didn't have any arguments with it, except that it was under someone else's watch. "If I say *no*?"

"You can go back to the motel. Fuck—you can walk out the front door alone, if you'd like."

That didn't sound right. "I thought there were orders from the top to keep me safe. And the promise you made Alex."

"I'll take the heat for letting you go, and if you're miserable, I haven't kept my promise anyway."

More freedom meant more chances to run, and so far, though Hare made her pulse race and her head spin, he'd never threatened her. "All right."

She felt like she was signing away a piece of her life she didn't understand, but deciding was better than sitting and waiting for something to happen.

Chapter Thirteen

Hare's idea of getting Reagan someplace safe was to hop on a private jet waiting for them at the municipal airport.

She sat in the back seat of the car and eyed the small plane with suspicion. "I'm not going to the Dominican Republic." She kept her tone light, but she was prepared to put her foot down if that was his actual plan.

He helped her from the car and pointed her toward the stairs leading up. "Seattle. That's where my condo is."

"Oh." She didn't trust him, but if he intended to hurt her, he was going to a lot of effort. Though maybe that was part of the game. "I don't think that's a good idea."

Hare's shoulders slumped. "You're not happy here, because you're too close to the danger. You don't want to be left alone. You don't want to be cooped up in a motel room. And now you're hesitating to get out of town. What do you think the right answer is?"

"Seattle sounds great." It didn't, but he had a

point about her options.

The trip was the most calming thing she'd done all week. In the air, she didn't have to worry about who wanted to talk to her, who was watching her room, or if she needed to be looking over her shoulder for a gunman. Hare told her to get some sleep, and for the first time in days, it felt all right to do so.

It wasn't that she trusted him any more than before, but there were fewer variables here, and if harm was his intent, she didn't think he'd get his kicks offing her in her sleep, after all the trouble he'd gone through.

She closed her eyes and let sleep overtake her.

It felt like only a few seconds later someone was shaking her awake. "Reagan." Hare's voice was soft. "We're landing."

She struggled to climb back to consciousness.

"Are you all right?" He studied her with concern.

"Tired. Did you slip me something?"

His smile was thin. "That's not the kindest assumption. You'd have needed to take a drink from me, for that to happen. I'm guessing you're tired."

"Yeah. That makes sense." She half-stumbled to the private runway and into the waiting car. She tried to stay awake on the drive, to take in the new city. It was too dark to enjoy, and she dozed in and out on their journey.

"Come on, sleepy." Hare wrapped an arm around her waist, and she leaned into him on the elevator ride up.

Bleary eyes kept her from appreciating the apartment, and when he pointed her toward a bed, she collapsed on top without even taking off her shoes.

She woke up the next morning to sun streaming over her face through slats in the blinds. She should feel bad about letting her guard down all night, but she needed to recover sometime. Fortunately, her instincts had served her.

A note sat on the nightstand. She grabbed it.

I had to work. Make yourself at home. You've got free reign of the place. I'll see you in a few hours. Hare.

A quick glance around the condo showed his taste—or his decorator's—was simple but expensive. A lot of black, white, and polished steel. The only art on the walls consisted of generic shapes in bright colors. She was tempted to slide into the freestanding tub in the guest bathroom and soak for an hour. After she finished her self-guided tour.

She hesitated at a door that was slightly ajar, then nudged it open. It had to be his bedroom. It felt like an invasion, stepping into someone else's private space.

He said free reign.

She'd take a peek, then go shower.

The room was as devoid of personal touches as the rest of the house, except for the faint scent of his cologne lingering in spots. She paused in front of his dresser, and a tiny sob rose in her throat. He had two framed pictures on top. One of him with an older woman—his mother, maybe—and the second of him with Alex.

She reached for the black frame, then pulled her hand back. Shaking her head, she forced herself to turn away, rather than fall into a spiral of memories.

As she spun, her gaze fell on a desk at the far side of the room. An open laptop decorated it. When Hare said *make yourself at home*, did it include this?

She didn't care. If there were answers on there about him, she wanted them. If not, she could spend some time digging through forums and keep an ear out for him.

Her pulse throbbed in her ears as she sat in the chair. She hovered her fingers over the keys. Guess his password and risk getting locked out? No. She needed an alternative way in. If she could get to a command prompt, she could look at files, but that would do her no good if he encrypted his data. And why wouldn't he?

His data was a bonus, though. She wanted to go online more than anything. Maybe she didn't need his machine. She had her phone. Without a SIM card, she couldn't get on a calling network, but she still had Wi-Fi.

She'd start there and come back here later. She hopped to her feet and spun.

Hare stood in the doorway. "Password is IMGod."

"Holy fuck. You scared me." Should she apologize for invading his space? How long was he watching her?

"You didn't wait long to sate your curiosity." He smiled. "There's hope for you yet. But you need to pay better attention to your surroundings."

"I'm sorry. I shouldn't have pried."

"Don't apologize if you don't mean it. I would have done the same. I wouldn't have gotten caught, though."

She stepped toward him. "I'll give you your room back."

"Join me for brunch?" He nodded toward the dining room.

If her life wasn't on the line, she'd be reluctant to leave this someone-else-foots-the-bill-for-everything behind when it was all over. Whenever that happened. "All right."

Conversation was sparse while they ate. She wasn't sure what to say, and he didn't offer any openings. Despite his calm approach, she still felt like she'd been caught misbehaving in his room.

Something new bothered her, though. It was a tiny thing, which made it a pleasant change of pace. "Your password isn't really IMGod," she said as they moved into the living room. She sat on the couch, and he took the spot next to her, turned sideways to face her.

"No. But I am a fan of the classics."

"*Hackers* isn't classic anything except trash," she said with a playful smile.

"One woman's trash is another man's treasure. *Hackers, Unusual Suspects, Unbroken*… Hell, anything M. Night Shyamalan."

"Not *Signs*. Or really anything that came after." She wrinkled her nose in distaste.

"Once again, to each their own. Besides, it's not about the details; it's the message."

"What kind of message is in *Hackers*? Chaos

saves the day?"

He rested his arm on the back of the couch and leaned in. "Giant corporations are driven by, grow by, and in the end are crushed by greed."

That was a sentiment she agreed with, but— "I wouldn't expect that from someone like you."

"Why not?"

"The organization you work for. Jabberwock makes his money playing middle-man to the same wealthy people who own those corporations." Emotion leaked into her voice. Passion and venom. She willed herself to have this conversation objectively. "His deals pay your check. Hell, you make a lot of those deals happen."

"*Guilty as charged* to all of the above, and yes, greed is a motivation. So is chaos. So is undermining that structure." His words flowed smoothly, as if he'd practiced them.

"By *undermining*, you mean *ensuring he has his fingers in everyone's pie*." Heat flooded her face, and she ducked her head. "That's not what I meant."

He tucked her hair behind her ear. "I know what you meant. Do you remember what I told you last night?"

"You told me a lot of things."

"I'm glad you were listening." He rolled his eyes, but he was smiling. "Deconstructing a person's beliefs takes time. I'm not going to argue Jabberwock's intentions with you. I'll tell you how it is, and if you're not ready to hear it, I'll stop." His statement triggered a thought she couldn't quite grasp.

She reached deep in her brain, tugged, and

hoped that what spilled out made sense. "What else are you holding back because you think I'm not ready?"

"So, so much. And yet, not nearly as much as you think." Hare stood. "I'm hoping you'll figure out some of it on your own."

"It might be easier if you just told me."

"Not these things, it wouldn't. I have to get back to work. Wi-Fi password is G0F1sh, capitalized, with a one and a zero. Your phone will connect."

"Don't walk out in the middle of this conversation." Her words landed against his back, and then the door, as it closed behind him. She flopped back on the couch with a grunt. "Fucking hell."

She gripped resolve and pushed it through her. The bath could wait. If he wanted her to find something, she would. She headed back into the guest room. Her purse sat on the nightstand, and she grabbed her phone from it.

Half an hour later, she'd done a patchwork root on the device—accessing the files to do the root as best she could, without hooking it up to an external machine—and downloaded a Tor client. First on her list was *Blake Allen*. Her searches alternated between following breadcrumbs sprinkled by Google, and digging through the deep web.

It took several attempts to verify she had the right guy, but she found and followed a link back to his driver's license. It didn't go anywhere. Not anyplace significant anyway. He had a couple of credit cards without a balance, a degree from an online college, and a high-school diploma. That was it. No lease or mortgage. No utility bills or car registration. No other past.

Even image searches returned nothing. That defied bizarre. No one could hide themselves that well. Once upon a time, maybe, but with the new ID systems in place, no one could hide completely.

As she dug, the light outside shifted and faded.

"Dinner?" Hare's call carried through her door.

She barely registered the question.

"Reagan?"

"Fine, thanks." The snippet of conversation drifted to the back of her mind. She didn't pay attention to the time, until she realized she was rubbing her eyes to see her screen in a dark room.

She moved to *Hare* next. Not that she expected to find anything about him. With only a name and a few photos…

Reagan let out a quiet *yes*, when an image search returned results. She sifted through photos. Some were with Alex and people she didn't recognize. A handful were with senators, CEO's, and prime ministers.

She stared at the images, puzzled. Hatter's existence had all but been erased, so why wasn't Hare's? It made her wish she'd snapped a photo of Dormouse when she had the chance.

But she didn't need to. Her hope for answers grew when she found a shot with Hare in the foreground and Dormouse hidden behind other people. It was grainy, but it should work.

Her elation was short-lived when the only results that returned were assorted sizes of the same picture. Reagan rubbed her eyes, to restore moisture to them. She should take a break soon.

She woke up the next morning with her phone screen stuck to her cheek and an ache behind her eyes. The tempting aroma of coffee floated to her. She let her nose guide her. When she opened her bedroom door, a set of shopping bags greeted her. New clothes. Again. If he kept this up, she'd never again have to wear the same outfit more than once.

Hardly something she'd sell her soul or sacrifice her freedom for, but a couple perks were nice.

She didn't see Hare, as she fixed herself a cup of coffee. A sip of the liquid helped her climb closer to *intelligent* and told her it was made less than an hour ago.

She took a quick shower and returned to her research. A few hours in, and she was no closer than yesterday. Besides the tidbits she'd snagged, she was as far away from an answer as when she and Wayne started searching.

What was she missing? She flopped back onto the mattress and scrubbed her face.

Rumors.

Thanks, brain. That was vague. The word bounced in her head, taunting her. No, it was perfect. Jabberwock was a man who had built his empire on reputation. His name—his infamy—was dependent on rumors. That meant she shouldn't be looking for facts; she should be paying attention to what people were saying.

She followed the trail to forums. It didn't matter if the source was reputable or not. She wanted to find where the stories overlapped. That would be where elements of the truth lay.

When her stomach growled at her around three-thirty, she realized she hadn't eaten lunch or heard from Hare. She grabbed a box of crackers, a jar of peanut butter, and a can of soda from the kitchen, dumped the now-cold coffee, and headed back to her room.

It was funny—for as much as she wanted out of her motel a few days ago, now this spot—this— bed, seemed safe. It was the closest thing she had to home base.

She absentmindedly munched while she hopped from one post to the other. She needed something to write on. Paper. She found a notepad and pen in the desk drawer. Thank God for people who decorated down to the last detail.

Each whisper that appeared more than once, even if the details were different, she scribbled on paper. Her eyes protested at the full day of staring at the tiny screen, and she lay back on the bed, blinking several times to find the energy to stare a little longer. She was so close. She could feel it.

Chapter Fourteen

Reagan picked her way along a dirt path overgrown with wildflowers. The taller weeds snagged her skirt, the same one she'd worn to the VR sex club. She pushed the fabric down, to keep the local foliage from stealing it.

A chorus of voices drifted from farther down the way, and she followed the sound. The plant life receded as she drew closer. She looked around, to get her bearings. It was sunflowers and lilacs, as far as she could see. She glanced down. Not only did she wear the skirt from the club, she had the whole outfit on.

She reached a clearing with a large oval table in the center. Hatter sat at the far end, top hat tilted to the side and tie crooked. Hare was across from him, dressed similarly, but without the hat. Dormouse was closer to Reagan, back ramrod straight and legs crossed. She even held her pinkie up while she sipped her tea.

"Alice," Hatter cried when he saw her. He pulled out a nearby chair and gave a deep bow. "Come. Join us. We're discussing philosophy."

"*They're* discussing philosophy." Dormouse poured something from a teapot. The black liquid almost oozed into her cup, and the scent—burnt coffee?—scorched Reagan's sinuses.

Reagan took the offered spot, next to Hatter. "What's the specific topic of discussion?" she asked.

"Why is a raven like a writing desk?" Hatter recited as if he was a book character.

She stared at him. *Seriously?* "Because they both have quills."

"*Ha.*" Hare slammed his palms on the table, and the china jumped. "I told you she was clever."

Reagan shook her head. "Wow. You people really take this Alice-in-Wonderland thing seriously. Hard core LARP-ers would envy your dedication."

"Making people believe is important." Hatter stood, wobbled on his feet, then collapsed in his chair again.

Hare nodded. "Faith is everything."

"It's not a religion. And it's not even your fetish." Reagan had a lot of outstanding questions but never expected to have to explain something like this. At least the entire universe had finally flipped on its head. "It's Jabberwock's. Isn't it?"

"It is." Hare circled the table and sat on the edge, close enough his knee brushed her arm. "What makes you think he's not here?"

The simple question made her skin crawl, and she cast her gaze around. If this was a movie or cartoon, she'd expect dark clouds and ominous music to accompany the question. "I only see the three of you."

Hare traced his finger over her bottom lip,

then poked her nose. "There are four of us. Never count yourself out. Maybe he's you. Maybe he's me." He looked at Hatter. "Definitely not him, though. He's got a different secret."

A jumble of conversations slammed into Reagan's thoughts, and her head throbbed. She pressed her palm to her forehead, but it didn't relieve the pain. Hare's voice echoed in her memory. A medley of every conversation they'd had. Of things Alex said to her.

Reagan sat up in bed with a start, clarity spilling in with consciousness. "Weird fucking dream." Telling her room made the experience no less odd. She glanced at the clock. Almost three in the morning. She faced forward again, and her neck protested, the pain jolting to her skull. She shouldn't have fallen asleep at such an odd angle.

Hare had to be home by now, most likely asleep, but she needed to talk to him.

She padded across the carpet and to his room. The door was ajar, light from the outside spilling through the balcony and painting a triangle on his carpet. He slept on his side, back to the door.

She crept toward him, the noise in her head screaming and bouncing around. When she reached the bed, she bent at the waist, to shake him awake.

The moment her fingers touched his arm, he jerked away, rolled onto his back, leveled a gun at her chest, and thumbed off the safety.

"It's me." Her words came out as a squeak, and she held up her hands.

He stared at her for several seconds. Could he hear her heart beating? It competed with the lingering traces of her odd dream—which didn't seem as surreal as it should, now that she was awake.

"What?" he finally said.

"It's you, isn't it? You're *him*." It wasn't one thing that tipped her off. He always knew too much. Had information from Jabberwock before there should be enough time to retrieve it. Had access to resources even Blake didn't.

Unlike Hatter and Dormouse, he never had to ask permission. Never seemed to doubt he was in the right. But why would he, if he was the man giving the orders?

He lowered the pistol, replacing the safety as he moved, and sat up. He extended his hand in greeting. "Pleasure to meet you, my dear."

Chapter Fifteen

Reagan lunged for the gun, but he was closer and faster.

He covered it with his hand, gaze never leaving hers. "You wound me." He frowned. "I thought you came in here to talk."

"*Talk?* Good word. Say a bunch of things—mean something completely different. Fuck with my head until I don't know *up* from *down*. Sure. We should *talk*. Let's start with what you prefer to be called." She saw the deception and half-truths from the start, but the optimistic part of her assumed it was because of who he worked for, not that he was the man everyone else worked for.

"I'm pretty fond of *Hare*. Jabberwock is a bit menacing for everyday conversation, don't you think?" He patted the mattress. "Sit. Relax. Let's sort this out."

"I'll stand. Thanks." She was never relaxing again. An ache formed behind her ribs. She'd tried to stay removed. Told herself he was full of shit and was keeping important things from her. But she'd fallen into the odd little trap he drew her into.

Trapped wasn't even the right word. She walked into this willingly. Every step of the way, he gave her a choice, and she always picked him—the man who thought it was fun to raise and fell empires.

The man who killed her brother.

Fuck. Her legs wobbled, and she locked her knees, to keep from toppling. Everything he said at the club, about him and her brother being close… "Did you even care about Alex?"

"Yes." A shadow settled in across his face, clear even in the dim light. "He was more my brother than he ever was yours."

"You fucking asshole." She wanted to hit him or find a way to get to that gun and shoot him, or something. Instead, like every other time she wanted out since this started, she stood there.

"Me? You didn't know him. He pulled down the moon and stars to keep you happy and from finding out what he was doing. And when I said he was the best, it was mild praise."

This was what she'd wanted. The entire reason she started down this path. If Hare—Jabberwock—was going to tell her the truth about one thing, she'd make it this. "Then why isn't he here now?"

"Because some things can't be stopped, no matter how much you want them to."

"*No*." She stomped her foot. She didn't care that it was childish or that he could level the pistol at her at any moment. "No more vague, distracting, not-quite answers. Tell me why Alex is dead, if he was so important to you both in business and personally?"

"He was embezzling from me. It wasn't a lot.

He skimmed a couple thousand dollars here and there, and I was willing to wait him out. See if he owned up to it. I'm not certain why he did it, but I suspect that was something the two of you had in common. The thrill and rush are driving motivations."

She clenched her jaw but wouldn't rise to the taunt.

Hare shrugged. "I let it slide until I couldn't anymore. Dormouse figured out what he was doing, and that's the kind of thing that can't go unanswered. If people hear I let it slide once, chaos ensues."

"I thought you liked chaos."

He gave her a dry smile. "Not like this. You would have been proud of him. At the very least, you should be grateful. He didn't beg. He didn't feed me an apology he didn't mean. There was a request, and that was it—to keep you safe."

"You've done a shit job."

"Have I? You're still here, aren't you? And— fuck—you're a pain in the ass. But you're also sexy, fun in bed, and intelligent. So it evens out."

"Don't shift the focus." Tears tried to spill out. She wouldn't let them. She wasn't sure if they were frustration or grief or pain, but they'd wait until she was alone. "There are a million ways you could have *kept me safe*. Why pull me into this world?"

"I didn't do that. Hatter's other employer did. You're giving me a lot more credit than I deserve, and I'm flattered, but I need to share the appreciation. If it helps you feel any better, what he'll suffer for betraying me is far worse than Alex's fate."

"No. It doesn't." She wanted to sink to the

floor, pull her knees to her chest, and rock until this went away. "Who does Hatter work for?"

"He didn't tell you? I was hoping he would. I don't know who else signs his checks, but you're also good bait, so I'll know soon enough." He winced. "That came out wrong. I didn't mean you're—"

"You did. You're using me to draw him out. That's a funny way to define *safe*. I'm done here." She should stay. Find out how much more he'd tell her while he was in this kind of honest mood, but the conversation was slipping, and if she didn't leave soon, she'd break in front of him. That wasn't an option.

"Reagan, come on. We're talking."

She stormed from his room, paused in hers to grab her purse and phone and slip on shoes, and walked out the front door. A sliver of satisfaction mingled with doubt and terror, when she slammed the door in his face and stalked toward the staircase.

As she burst into the stairwell, that familiar surge of adrenaline kicked in, pumping through her veins and pulsing in her legs. She sprinted down the stairs, eager to get to the bottom. To be outside. It didn't matter it was before four in the morning. Odds were few people knew she was here, she had the cash Hare had so generously supplied her with, and she needed to run.

She stepped out the back door of the building and paused. Maybe she should've figured out the lay of the neighborhood first. Great. She'd spent days letting herself be the princess, locked away in a labyrinth of lies, and now she was the too-stupid-to-live adventurer.

This was a city. There would be a convenience store somewhere, where she could buy a burner phone. Something that let her place calls and couldn't be traced to her. She'd pick a direction and walk until she found an indicator of where to go next.

Someone grabbed her arms hard enough to send a jolt of pain rocketing through her shoulders, and something rough and cottony was stuffed in her mouth before she could scream. Her heart kicked into overdrive when a cloth bag was pulled over her head, tight enough to hold the gag in place.

She struggled to catch her breath, but every new drag through her nose left her feeling as if she suffocated. The fabric covering her face was musty, and whatever was in her mouth sapped moisture away.

Reagan kicked off the ground, trying to throw whoever held her off balance. Their grip tightened, and a second set of hands grabbed her ankles and shoved them toward her chest. She tried to scream, but all that came out was a muffled squeak. The harder she twisted and turned, the tighter they held her.

Her world bounced. They were moving. Seconds later, she hit the ground, jarring her shoulder into her jaw. Ignoring the pain, she tried to shoot to her feet, but a hand at her neck shoved her back down, and her arms were yanked behind her back.

Cold, smooth metal bound her wrists, and a similar sensation tingled around her ankles. She heard the clink of a chain, and her arms and legs were jerked back. She struggled for all she had, but the angle they'd shackled her to the floor made it tough to move, and each squirm squeezed a tighter fist around her lungs, until she gasped for air she couldn't find.

An engine roared to life, and she was jostled when the grounded jerked beneath her. *Fucking hell, I'm moving.* The tears she held back earlier surged forward. When she tried to sob, her gag did its job, and she fell into a fit of choking coughs that racked her body and throbbed in her shoulder, hip, and skull.

Stay calm. She could do that. It took several minutes, but she forced herself to breathe through her nose, slow and even, until her heart rate slowed to something beneath galloping. *Now relax.* Okay. If she could find a position that didn't cramp her muscles, she'd have another chance to catch them off guard and break free when they stopped.

The way she was bound made getting comfortable impossible. It took immense force of will to keep her muscles from cramping. She didn't know if it was better or worse that sleep spread from her foot and up her leg, leaving the limb numb.

She didn't know how long they drove. She tried counting seconds in her head, but kept losing track before she reached five minutes. For all she knew, they were in Portland. Or Canada. Okay, probably not Canada. Someone would want to search back here, right? And they hadn't been driving all day. It had to have been an hour or two.

The ground stopped moving, like it had countless times already, but this time the engine shut off. She squirmed and banged her leg against the floor. *Wake up, please.*

Hinges creaked, and the air pressure changed.

At least two people held her hands and legs, while she was unlocked from the chains holding her to the floor. Pins and needles shot through her calf.

The way they carried her, she couldn't twist away, and not for lack of trying. She was set on the ground, more gently this time. The second the cuffs feel away from her legs and arms, she thrashed out wildly. She connected with something and heard a satisfying *oof.* She scrambled to her feet, but stumbled when she tried to put her weight on her legs. She landed on her ass, and agony rocketed up her spine into her skull.

She yanked the sack from her head, and the gag less than a second later, and took in her surroundings.

Not that there was much to see. The walls and floor were unpainted concrete. There was no window. A mattress sat on the floor in the corner, and a stainless-steel toilet was bolted to the wall. The door was painted to match the concrete and looked metal, with no lock or latch inside.

"*Hey,*" she screamed, and her voice echoed back at her. "*Hello?*" No answer. No sound outside the door. Nothing.

"*Hey. Let me out. Talk to me.*" She pounded on the door. Still nothing. Her earlier panic surged back, fresh and gnawing. She yelled and hammered until her hands throbbed and her throat was raw.

Nothing. She sank to the floor and pulled her knees to her chest. *Don't cry. It won't help.* Neither did anything else. She sobbed in the barren room, and the walls bounced the sound back to taunt her.

Chapter Sixteen

Reagan cried until her eyes burned and she was gasping through sniffles. It didn't change anything, but she felt cleansed in an odd way. As she let focus spill back into her senses, she realized the walls weren't as smooth and barren as she originally thought. There was a square in one corner of the ceiling that reflected light back at her. She stood and wandered to it. It looked like glass and was maybe six inches square. A camera? She couldn't tell. The light in the room kept her from seeing what lay on the other side, but *camera* seemed like as reasonable a guess as anything.

What else did she miss when she arrived? She searched the room again—not that it took long. There was a patch in the wall across from the bed. A rectangle about two feet wide. She tapped it with her knuckles, and a hollow, metal sound greeted her. She knocked the wall outside the square to confirm. Yup. Concrete.

There was another rectangle on the same wall as the large one, almost as wide but only about six inches tall and just above her waist level.

Is this Hare's doing? His response to her decision not to roll over and wait for life to pass her by? He obviously enjoyed the mind fuck. Was this another one of his games?

"*Hello.*" Her call rang in her ears.

Nothing.

She wasn't going to scream herself hoarse this time. If they could hear her, they already had. She turned to the glass in the ceiling. If it was a camera, and there was a mic in the room, they were watching and listening. If not, no one would know she was about to bargain with an empty room.

"Anyone there?" Reagan asked the piece of glass. "If this is something Jabberwock ordered"—a shudder of betrayal shook her body, and she forced it down—"I'm willing to admit I was unreasonable. I'm happy to talk this out with whomever you want to send in, like a rational adult."

Minutes ticked away. Nothing.

"Hello?" She let frustration bleed into her voice.

The sound of a motor filled the room, and the larger square on the wall slid open. The screen beneath flickered to life, and she jumped at the abrupt volume of the news program it played.

"*Hey.* Can I get the sound cranked down? Maybe change the channel to some *Big Brother*?" She couldn't help a dry smile at her joke. If no one else was here to be amused at how clever she was, she'd do it.

The news rolled on without change. It was an old clip she'd seen several times, because it was about the CEO of a tech company who died under suspicious circumstances. Rumors said Jabberwock had him killed.

The segment reached its conclusion, and she waited, curious for what came next. The sound died, and a photo flashed on the screen. She squinted for a moment. *Oh God.* It was a photo of a gunshot exit wound, detailed and up close. Bile rose in her throat, and she choked it back down. The next image was another angle, wider, of a crime scene. The surroundings were the CEO's home, the room where his body had been found.

Unlike other photos Reagan had seen, his body was still in these. The next was another up-close photo, and so was the fourth. She heaved and forced her gaze from the screen.

Jabberwock rarely pulled the trigger himself, because he stayed hidden, but that didn't mean he was any more innocent in this or other crimes. Then again, given that he masqueraded as one of his own generals, he might be doing as much killing as anyone.

Having been shot at after Wayne's funeral, she thought she understood how serious this was. But with each new reality shoved in her face, another layer of security was stripped from her. Hare— Jabberwock—the man she'd let lead her around for almost a week and never really hesitated to fuck, was responsible for these things. These brutal, horrific things. Did Alex look like that when he died?

Was that what she was meant to understand? Did Hare toss her in here to drive his point home? Was he this off his rocker? The question didn't taste right, and she laughed at herself. She was defining how bad *bad* was? Painting gray areas between ordering people killed and tossing her in a cell to teach her a lesson?

The photos of the CEO faded, and another news story started. The volume was as loud as before, jarring her and drawing her gaze.

It was a clip she'd seen before, but the first time, she watched it with subtitles. It was in Spanish, about a coup in Venezuela. This time a news anchor screamed at her in a language she didn't speak. As the story came to an end, another video started; a shaky, handheld shot. She recognized the clip from YouTube. It was about the same revolt.

Again, still photos with no sound followed. Rows of bodies lined up on the street, some covered with sheets and others exposed. The wounds were worse than the CEO's. Burns. Splintered limbs. So much death and pain.

She squeezed her eyes shut and looked away. "I get it," she shouted. "You're a big badass who makes corporations and countries rise and fall. You can't be fucked with. *I get it*," she repeated.

The volume kicked on again, and she pressed her hands to her ears, to block out the sound. Her stomach growled. What time was it? She didn't eat much yesterday. Was starving her part of whatever this was?

The news continued in the background, but she kept her gaze focused on the door. With her ears plugged, she heard the shifts in volume from blaring to nothing but blocked out most of the details.

After about two dozen blinks between loud and quiet, she caught a movement out of the corner of her eye. The smaller opening in the wall was open—it was like a passthrough from another room. Inside sat two bottles of water, and a foil packet.

Don't listen. She dropped her fingers from her ears and crossed the room to examine the goods.

The water was in sealed bottles. She cracked one and downed half of it in a swig. The room-temperature liquid hit her empty stomach with a *thud*, and she forced herself to pause, rather than getting sick.

She fought back a smile when she examined the large packet had written on the top, in large black letters, *Meal, Ready-to-Eat*. Alex always brought MRE's when he took her camping. It meant the food was probably safe and mostly edible, and she could make it last if she needed. She tore into the packet, and picked out the fruit. She wanted to eat the entree, but she'd save that.

She took her time. Focusing on eating made it easier to drown out the TV, and let her slide into some of the happier memories about Alex—the things he used to drill into her head when he'd do things like take her camping. For instance, to never eat the food or drink the water unless it's prepackaged. Back then, she teased him about being paranoid. Was he prepping her for something like this?

With some sugar and sustenance racing in her veins, her head was working better. She settled onto the mattress, back against the far wall, and got as comfortable as she could with the news blaring.

It was tempting to grab the sack-blindfold from the floor where she'd left it, roll it up so it would only cover her eyes and ears, and use it to block out the light and sound. Maybe she could doze, in that case.

But the thought of putting that thing back on squeezed the breath from her lungs. It was better this way. She needed to stay aware of her surroundings.

Reagan studied her feet, rather than letting the images on the TV offer up new and creative nightmares. Her eyelids grew heavy, and she pinched her cheeks to try and stay awake. She had no idea what time of day it was, but she hadn't slept since the odd dream at Hare's condo.

She was startled awake by a sharp scream. She looked at the TV, pulse shredding through her. The image that played out was grainy but steady. A cheap camera on a tripod, maybe. The noise was a woman—girl?—backed in a corner. Three young men laughed and jeered as they took turns forcing themselves on the disheveled woman.

Reagan wanted to look away, but horror held her attention. Was this a veiled threat? A *you're next* kind of thing? The rapists finished, and the girl curled into a small ball, sobbing. Reagan finally managed to stop watching. She was going to be ill.

"What the fuck is wrong with you?" The familiar female voice drew Reagan's gaze, and despite the voice in her head screaming *don't look*, her head jolted up again.

Dormouse was on the screen. One of the guys opened his mouth to speak, and Dormouse leveled her pistol and shot him in the head. Before the other two could move, she'd delivered them the same fate.

Dormouse was a good fucking shot. And

Reagan's respect and appreciation for the general rose several points.

The conclusion to the film didn't erase the victim's screams or her assailants' laughs from Reagan's thoughts. Sickness surged forward, and she lunged for the toilet. Several minutes of retching later, what she'd emptied the contents of her stomach.

The toilet flushed on its own. *At least I have modern conveniences.* The sarcastic thought didn't reassure her.

She pressed herself back into the corner, sitting on the mattress, watching the door, singing songs, reciting poems—anything that came to mind, to block out the TV.

She was so tired. Each time she dozed, the TV woke her up. And then the original story played again. They had it on a loop. Could she use the clips to get some idea of passage of time? Nothing related to the real world, but to be able to say she was on the second loop or the third would be *something*.

Except the next video wasn't the one from Venezuela. And then ran one she hadn't seen. And the original played twice in a row. And whoever had her in here really liked the fucking execution clip with Dormouse—that was the only way Reagan could let herself think about it.

Exhaustion finally won out, and she slept. She had no idea how long for, but when she woke up, she was lying down and her neck was stiff.

The familiar whirring noise of a motor drew her attention, and the smaller slot opened again.

"Trash goes in the slot." The digital voice

overlapped the TV. Most likely words spoken by the computer after someone input them.

She looked at the camera. "What if I don't?"

There was a few seconds' pause. "Then you don't get more."

No reason to test her fate when it came to food and water. She peered in the hole. It ran deep enough she couldn't see the other end. She was tempted to put her arm in and see what she could feel, but she'd experiment first.

She placed both bottles in but left one sticking out. Just the neck. Hopefully something the camera wouldn't be able to see.

"Better?" she asked.

The motor whirred. The door slid down and sliced through the neck of the bottle without a pause. Reagan picked up the severed plastic from the ground, and swallowed hard at the clean, precise cut.

When the compartment opened again, there were two more bottles of water in there, but no food this time. She was glad she hadn't eaten all of hers yet.

Time ticked away, measured in videos. Water came twice as often as food. She grabbed naps when she could. If she thought being stuck in a motel room was boring, this was going to drive her out of her fucking mind.

She couldn't sit in here and rot. She'd do pushups, but her arms weren't strong enough. Maybe it was time to learn. Whoever was watching could laugh at her wimpiness, and if they left her in here too long, she'd be Sara Conner. But from *Terminator 2*, not the first one.

She pushed off the wall rather than the floor, because she wasn't Sara Conner yet. Ten. Then twenty. Sweat trickled down her back. She wasn't exerting herself that much. She kept going. *It's hot in here.* She had to stop before her arms were tired, because her palms were so slick with sweat.

Great. Not only was she stuck in the same clothes she had when she left Hare's, she was also gross and sweaty on top of that. She sat again and sipped water until her body temperature returned to normal.

A new clip blared onto the screen. The date on it was recent. The day after she left Hare's. The piece was about a condominium fire in downtown Seattle.

Her stomach dropped into her shoes. She was almost certain that was Hare's building. "What the fuck is this?" she screamed.

Nothing.

Clips bled together. She fell asleep and woke up shivering. She tried to exercise, and the heat in the room rose probably twenty degrees. She crammed one of her meals down the toilet and tried to flood the room. Would someone come running?

The water spilled across the floor. They hadn't shut off the source yet. Maybe they weren't watching her that closely? The water level only reached a few millimeters in the room. She realized it was escaping through tiny vents at the bottom of the walls.

"Clear the clog yourself, or you won't have a toilet," the mechanical voice said.

"Are you kidding?"

The computerized voice repeated its message.

Reagan rolled her eyes, fished out the soaked food, and tossed it in the open slot in the wall. She returned to her futon. As the room dried, a musty smell greeted her. The only thing she'd accomplished was making her mattress damp and smelly. Or maybe the stench was her. She didn't know anymore.

"Don't flush this one," the mechanical voice was back a few hours later, along with another MRE.

"Fine." She'd do one better. She tore the heating packet from her meal packet, and poured in enough water to get it hot. Then dumped the scalding water over her arm.

She screamed as the burning agony seared through her body. This might not be her smartest move to date, but logic wasn't doing her any good, so what the hell? They'd have to treat her if she was injured, right? She didn't hold back her whimpers and screams, letting them drown out the TV.

When the pain was too much to bear, she shoved her arm in the toilet and let the chilly water chase away the heat. At least temporarily. Blisters were forming on her skin.

She looked at the camera. "Do I have to kill myself to get a person in here?"

Chapter Seventeen

"Your safety isn't as important as mine." The familiar voice and words taunted Reagan. It was what her would-be kidnapper said when he approached her at the restaurant. "The gun is loaded, and if you scream, if you run, if you try to walk away from me, I *will* shoot you in the back."

The screen flickered to a news story she hadn't seen yet, featuring the gunman's body, lying in the parking lot where she and Hare left him. It was local Salt Lake News, and the scrolling headline says *John Doe found dead in Murray parking lot.* According to the anchorwoman, the police weren't releasing a cause of death, but they were looking for any information.

Hare had lied to her again. The gunman was dead, and Hare was the one who killed him.

"There's no scenario where you walk cleanly away from this." The digital voice was back. "You can break, or you can take the coward's way out."

"Break for *what*? I don't know what you fucking want!"

"The same thing you said you wanted."

"The fuck out of here? That's the only thing I want right now."

There was no response. She didn't know if it was worse that she argued with a computer, or that it was the one to end the conversation.

More time passed. Enough for another meal, and at least three-hundred more video and photo clips.

The door latch clicked, and her muscles tensed before her brain processed the sound. She looked around for a weapon, but of course, there was none. She'd kick someone if she had to. Even if they took her down, she'd feel a glimmer of satisfaction if she landed a nut shot.

Two men in full body armor burst into the room, shoulder to shoulder, assault rifles pointed at her. Their faces were hidden under helmets and black masks.

The guns made her hesitate. No. She didn't care. She'd rush one of them anyway, and see if she could catch them off guard.

"Stop." Blake stepped between them.

Rage and hurt flooded Reagan's limbs. She screamed and lunged. One of the guards sidestepped, tripped her, and landed a knee in the small of her back. He twisted her arm behind her back. A agony shot from the burns on her forearm all the way to her shoulder. She bit the inside of her cheek until she tasted copper. She wouldn't give them the satisfaction of crying out in pain.

"I said *stop*," Blake shouted. "What the fuck is wrong with you?"

"Sir?" the man pinning her down said.

Hearing human voices for the first time since she arrived set her brain off balance.

"She's a fucking guest"—anger dripped from Blake's words—"and you have her locked up like a terrorist."

"But we were told—"

"I don't care." Blake cut the other guard off. "Take her to a real room, get her a change of clothes, and let her shower."

Reagan let a bitter laugh slip out, as she was hauled to her feet. This was something else Alex taught her—how psychological torture worked. It was rarely about direct pain.

"Something funny, Alice?" Blake studied her.

"That's not my fucking name. But it's nice to know we're all mad here."

He raised his brows.

"This isn't going to work any better than anything else you've done to me."

"What won't?"

"This *good-cop, bad-cop* bullshit. Leave me in here if you're going to keep playing this psychological-warfare game."

Blake frowned and turned to the guard still at the door. "Real room. Now. Then I want you back in the vault."

He nodded, handed Blake his rifle, and stepped toward Reagan. Both guards were large enough that they kept her immobile while they put shackles on her legs and arms and connected the two sets behind her back.

"I thought I wasn't a prisoner." She let the

sarcasm drip from her voice.

"You're not allowed to walk out of here, regardless of your status. And I'm not going to lie to you about it, the way Jabberwock's people did—"

"You're one of those people."

"—but you're upper crust, not bottom rung." He kept talking as if she hadn't. "Besides, we need to relocate you with as few casualties as possible, to you or them."

She gave him a thin smile. "Swell."

He stepped aside, and she was led down a long hallway. When she stumbled, she was dragged until she caught her footing again. They stepped into an elevator and rode up to a floor labeled *P*. The new hallway was as nondescript as the old one. Another man waited at one of the doors. He kept his gun trained on her, while her shackles were removed.

The door was opened, and she was pushed inside.

It was almost identical to the motel room she'd spent several days locked in. She dropped to her knees, struggling to contain her frustration. The broken blisters on her arm throbbed in time with the ache in her skull.

When the door creaked open behind her, she couldn't find the desire to move.

"You were in there for a week." It was Blake. His voice, once friendly and familiar, grated against her nerves. "If they were going to torture you, they would have dragged it out a lot longer. And I wouldn't be a part of it."

She rolled her eyes. Lying fucking bastard. Hare was right; Hatter did have a second employer.

She dragged herself to her feet and turned to face him. "The non-stop abuse doesn't work in psychological torture, unless there's some nice sprinkled in. The hope of kindness. That taste of relief, before it's yanked away again. And according to the exchange downstairs, you weren't a part of it this time either. So… I'm not reassured."

"I don't blame you. I had no idea that was going on. I'm sorry."

"Hmm. I feel all better now. Thanks." She studied him. Slacks. A button-down shirt with the sleeves rolled halfway up his forearms. No tie. No shoulder- or hip-holster. Did he have a hidden one? No lump near his ankle.

He held his arms straight out and turned in a slow circle. "They didn't let me come in here armed. Pat me down if you'd like."

"I really wouldn't. I'm not sure why you came in here at all. And who are *they*?"

Blake raked his fingers through his hair and sighed. "Do you want to sit?"

"No."

"Suit yourself. *They* are Homeland Security. I'm with the National Security Agency, and helping them on this case."

Well, shit. She didn't see that coming. "Hare was right. You do have a second job." If she told these people who Jabberwock really was, they'd probably be pretty thrilled. And if they'd approached her politely, she might have considered it. After the past week, she needed something for collateral.

"*Had*," Blake corrected her. "They pulled me out, because somehow, Hare figured it out. I kind of hoped you and I had a rapport. An understanding. I didn't expect you to sell him my identity."

She snort-laughed. "Your people locked me in a cell for a week without any explanation, and *I'm* the one who broke the bonds of trust? I never told him anything, except that you and I were together the night Wayne died. I assumed Jabberwock sent you."

Pieces clicked in her head. If she told Hare, she told Jabberwock. If he didn't assign Hatter… Hare knew from the night in the country club that Hatter wasn't one of his after all. Technically she *was* the one who sold him out. She might feel worse about it if almost everything about this situation was different. "Wait. Is this place wired with cameras, like my other cell?"

"Yes."

"Do your employers know you fucked me that night in Las Vegas?" She let satisfaction glimmer inside when he winced.

"Yes."

"Was that part of the job?" she asked.

"Keeping you safe was. Wayne was our contact, so he tipped us off to your location, and watching you was for both him and the job. The sex only had to do with you and me."

"Ooh, I feel special now." She closed the distance between them. "Do you want to join me in the shower? Help me get clean? Show your colleagues what they missed out on, letting you keep an eye on me alone?" She asked in her sweetest voice.

Blake stepped back and scrubbed his face. "No."

"Then you'd better hurry to the camera room if you want to enjoy the show." She turned away, stripping off her shirt. She didn't care who saw her doing what, and if they had some sort of sick twist planned by letting her bathe, she'd experience it clean.

She heard Blake sigh, and a second later, her door opened and then latched shut.

An hour later—at least this room had a clock and a TV with a working remote—she lay on the bed, damp hair spread out around her as she stared at the ceiling. Her brain still felt like it had been forced through a cheese grater, but she smelled like flowers and cheap soap instead of like she'd been locked in a cell for a week in the same outfit. The clothes they left for her were hers, from her apartment. Which was another new kind of creepy. At least she got to explore a variety of flavors of disturbing.

Someone knocked.

"*Now* you bother with propriety?" she called. "Like I can stop you from coming in?"

Blake stepped into the room. "You're being held, but we're reasonable." He sounded tired.

She didn't feel the least bit sorry for him. "Reasonable. Right. Filming me while I shower and shit is completely rational." She sat up. At the same moment she saw the paper bag in his hand, grease staining one side, the smell of fast-food hamburgers and fries hit her. Her stomach churned in protest. "I'm not eating anything that's not pre-packaged."

"I don't blame you." He put the paper bag on

the edge of the dresser but still held two plastic bags. He set the first in front of her on the mattress. The sack held an MRE and a bottle of Gatorade.

He sat next to her on the mattress and unpacked the second bag. "We need to take care of that burn. How the hell did you do that, anyway?" He pulled out gauze, tape, and a tube of antibiotic ointment.

"Your watchdog friends didn't tell you?"

"Did they do it?" He reached for her arm.

She jerked away. "I did it. I wanted them to stop ignoring me."

"Fuck. I'm so sorry." He held out the ointment. "You can apply this yourself, but it's going to be easier if you let me help." His tone was sympathetic without the slightest edge.

She was too tired to argue. She shifted enough to give him better access to her arm. His touch, soft and tentative, dragged memories to the front of her mind. Of Las Vegas. Of the first night in the motel, after being shot at, when Hare washed off the scrapes on her legs. Her stomach churned at the thoughts

Her brain skipped over random events, treating her to an image of a man lying motionless in a parking lot, then patching in several stills from the videos she'd been shown downstairs. She shuddered.

"Are you all right?" Blake asked.

"Really? You think it's okay to ask me that? You don't know the answer?"

"You're right. I'm sorry." He covered the sores on her arm with salve, easing up each time she winced and waiting until she relaxed before resuming his doctoring. A few minutes later, he finished and scooted back on the mattress.

Decorum said she should thank him. *Fuck decorum.*

"Why am I here?" she finally asked. "Someone tried to shoot me. The same guy tried to take me. I'm guessing he's one of yours. And now I'm in your custody, because… Why?"

Blake drummed his fingers on his leg. "He was one of ours. That's part of the reason you got the treatment you did. Some of these guys blame you."

"Hare told me he was unconscious. I didn't know he was dead until I saw the news clip."

"I figured. You don't radiate *killer*. I'm still furious they did that to you. You're here because I've been inside Jabberwock's organization for seven years, and at the top for three. You—not the circumstances around you, but you personally—are the first time I've ever seen him uproot entire branches of his organization. He pulled half his people from their posts around the world to guard you, and has delayed dozens of deals since you stepped into the picture. He only stopped short of moving the world for you. We want to know why."

That didn't make any sense, even given what Hare told her about Alex. But if he had been using her as bait, turning things on their head was the perfect way to make a mole ask *why,* and throw them off their game. The way things crumbled for Hatter. "I don't know. I'm a college student who wanted to find out what happened to my brother. That's it. I'm nothing special," she said.

Blake looked up and caught her gaze.

Something in his eyes made her breath catch, but she didn't know what or why. "You're obviously someone special." Did his voice just crack?

No.

He stood and moved the remaining first-aid supplies to the nightstand. "Get some sleep. If you can. I need to find out what happens next."

"Will you share that information with me?"

He turned away.

She wasn't surprised by the lack of an answer.

Sleep wasn't happening. As minutes ticked into hours, a new plan formed. It was probably lunacy. It had a million points for failure. But she played it safe while Hare—that was still his name in her mind, regardless of what she knew—had her, and now she was here.

Blake returned at eight thirty the next morning, knocking again. Breakfast was a can of iced coffee and a pre-sealed container with grapes, cheese, and almonds. "I thought you might want something a little lighter," he said. "If you reach the point where you want specific food, let me know."

"Thanks. But I won't be here long enough for it to matter."

"Oh?" His hand flew to his hip, but there was no holster.

At least she knew where he kept his gun. And that he didn't trust her. Good to know that went both ways. "You're going to release me." She held up her hand when he opened his mouth. "Hear me out. You told me yesterday that Jabberwock upended his entire organization for me. You want to know why.

Let me go."

"We can't do that."

"I'm not staying here."

He frowned. "We can hold you indefinitely without charging you."

"What good does that do you?" she asked. "I don't know anything. I'm not important to you outside of whatever the fuck Jabberwock wants with me. Shoot me or release me. The way I figure it, if Jabberwock actually has any interest in me, the moment I'm back on his radar, he'll be following me again."

"And you think he'll retrieve you without hesitation, this man you've never met? He's going to be wary as fuck about wherever you vanished to."

"He will be. It's true. That's why you give me my distance, and let me work my way back in." Even if they did release her, she didn't think for a second that they'd take eyes off her, but she'd pretend. "If it makes you feel better, you can take the lead."

"He's definitely not going to approach you if you're with me," Blake said.

She flopped back onto the bed and turned her gaze to the ceiling. "That's my offer. Think it over. Talk to the people in charge."

"Ali— Reagan, this isn't going to fly."

She didn't respond. Hatter and Hare didn't get to be the only people who had secrets. Seconds ticked away, until she heard the door open and latch shut again.

Please let this get me out of here.

Chapter Eighteen

Despite telling herself she had a good plan, Reagan was surprised when Blake returned with an *okay*.

She was less than surprised when they handed back her purse minus the hundreds of dollars in cash that she'd had.

When she asked about it, Blake shrugged. "It was seized, having come from illegal sources. You said you could draw out Jabberwock's people. You never said anything about needing financing."

"Are you serious?"

His confident expression slipped. "This isn't my call. I had to beg, run this up to the top, and use your torture as leverage, and even then…" He looked away.

She didn't like that. "What?"

"If they think for a second that this has gone south, you're gone. I don't mean brought back here."

"Yeah. Dead. I get it." She swallowed past the lump in her throat. "Can I at least get a ride out of here?"

"Definitely." He held out a blindfold.

She was grateful it wasn't a sack this time.

That didn't stop a shudder of nausea from rolling through her, dragging back flashes of her time spent in the cell. "Are you serious?"

He shrugged. "We're secretive. Where do you want to go?"

"Depends on where I am."

He twisted his mouth.

Un-fucking-believable. "I'm going to figure out what city we're in when you drop me off, and unless we're on a border, I'll have a good idea of the state as well."

"You can pick any destination between Portland and Vancouver."

Perfect. She knew they were within a few hour's drive of Seattle, but the range he gave her put her back near Hare. If he was still there. She had to start someplace. "Drop me back where you found me."

"That's a burned-out husk of a condo. And also a little suspicious."

"The nearest grocery store, then." She let a grim smile leak out. Improbable Bullet Point One on her list was done, if she didn't count the looming executioner's ax. Time to see if the next one worked.

The drive didn't seem as long this time, but that might be because she was sitting in the back seat of a sedan, rather than chained to the floor. When Blake pulled the blindfold off, she saw it had been about three hours.

That could mean their *top-secret* location was three hours away, or simply that they drove her in circles for that long. But they weren't farther than that.

As they pulled into a grocery-store parking lot, she felt Blake's hand slide along her backside. She jolted her head up to look at him, and he made the slightest *shh* sound. "Your stop," he said at normal volume. "There's a Residence Inn a few blocks from there. If you check in there, and tell them you have a reservation under the name A.L. Bugs, we'll pick up the bill for your stay. We'll be in touch."

Seconds later, she stood on the curb, and her ride was gone.

She blinked several times in the afternoon light, trying to get her eyes to adjust. The roar of traffic, chatter of people, blare of horns, and squawk of birds drilled into her at once, until she didn't know where to look.

"Are you okay?" The question gave her focus, and she whirled to see an older woman studying her with concern.

Reagan smiled. "I'm fine, thank you." She wasn't in the mood to make conversation, though. "Have a lovely day." She spun away before the woman could say more, and shouldered her way into the store.

It hadn't been that long since she was around large crowds of people. Why did walking into a simple grocery store suck the breath from her and make her head spin?

She forced herself to calm. This was normal. It was everyday life. And the faster she got out of here, the better. She cut toward the service desk and took her spot in the line. Blake's odd behavior trickled in, and she reached into her back pocket.

He'd slipped her a card of some sort. She pulled it out. The small envelope looked like the kind gift cards came in. It contained a key, a debit card, and a business card with a note and an address.

They're watching you, not me. If you check into the hotel after 8 pm, and look for Gale she'll put you in a good room. The card has $500 on it. I'm sorry it's not more.

She didn't want the glimmer of appreciation that flitted through her, but she couldn't ignore it.

"Next."

Reagan stepped up to the clerk and summoned her warmest smile. "Is there any way I could use your phone?" Her excuse clung to the tip of her tongue. The story she'd tell… The pleading she'd do…

"Sure." He nodded to the next window over. "Dial *9* to get an outside line."

It took her a second to say, "Thanks." She moved to the store phone and dialed Mindy's number.

"Hello?"

Reagan's heart ached at the sound of the friendly, familiar voice. *I want to go home.* "Hey. It's me." She managed to keep her voice from cracking.

"Oh my God, Reagan. Where are you? Are you okay? What happened? Someone broke in and ransacked your room the day after you said you were going to that funeral, and I haven't heard from you in weeks."

"I'll explain it all soon, I promise." Reagan winced at the lie. "I need two favors, please. I wouldn't ask if I wasn't desperate."

"Of course. Anything."

"Can you wire me some money? Just a hundred bucks. I— I'm stuck in Seattle and I need to get home."

"What are you doing there?"

"When I get home. Please?"

"Sure. Of course. I'll go online as soon as we hang up."

Reagan let out a tiny sigh. "And one other thing. There's a shortcut on your laptop. It says Tor on it."

"What did you install on my computer?" Mindy asked.

"It's a web browser. No big deal. The shortcut should take you to a message board. I need you to post something that says *Alice is looking to join a tea party.*" It didn't matter that she never told Hare what Wayne called her. If Mindy used the icon Reagan set up, the message wouldn't have the right encryption. The note would trace back to her old address, and the wire transfer would trace to this store, and her ID.

"No," Mindy said.

"Excuse me?"

"You vanish off the face of the planet for days, call me from four states away, and ask for money. Okay, fine. But now you want me to help you chase this bullshit phantom of Wayne's?"

"Please?" Reagan forced a hint of sob into the word.

"All right. But you owe me."

"I know I do. Thank you," Reagan said.

It only took fifteen minutes for Reagan to get her money. She didn't have anything to after that except wait for Jabberwock to send someone for her.

She strolled town, and wandered into a library. The quiet was soothing. As she meandered through the shelves, she grabbed random books and read the backs.

After that, she found a Chinese restaurant a few blocks from the grocery store, and stopped for an early dinner. It felt odd, sitting down alone to eat but being surrounded by so many faces. Were any of them Blake's colleagues? Was there a Four of Clubs in here somewhere, or a Two of Hearts?

She placed her order, then did a quick circuit of the place, memorizing exits. The restroom had a second door in back. Interesting. She'd check that out later if she had the chance.

At her table, she ordered, but when her food came, she hesitated to eat. Which was odd. It wasn't as though anyone had slipped anything into her meals before, and if she were being realistic, the people holding her could have drugged her in any number of ways outside of her food.

The logic didn't stop her from taking the first few bites slowly and waiting several minutes to makes sure she felt okay. When everything seemed in order, she dove into the rest of the dish.

She spent the time until nightfall wandering the city streets, adapting to the noise, and drowning in the crowds. She memorized the note from Blake, then burned it.

If Jabberwock's people were on her, the spooks she had following her would pick it up, but he was smarter than that. He'd watch until he knew he had a clear opening to her.

A little after nine, she found herself in front of the hotel Blake told her to go to. She couldn't explain to herself why she was accepting his invitation. She found Gale at the front desk. "I'm A.L. Bugs. I have a reservation for the night?"

The desk clerk's gaze flickered to Reagan for the briefest second. "Of course. Give me a minute… It looks like your room charges are covered. Here's your key. Room 210."

"Thank you." Reagan gave her a weak smile.

She took the stairs to the second floor. The way the building was laid out, if someone was following her, they'd see her go in, but not where she went, unless she saw them as well. No one followed her up. No one waited in the hallway when she emerged.

The room she was looking for was around the corner. She slid the key in the lock and pushed inside.

It was dark, except for a light above the stove in the kitchenette area. The blinds were drawn, blocking most of the light from the street. She turned on one light, but left the others out, liking the control she had over how much she saw.

Was it really her own room? She sat on the bed, knees together and fingers intertwined, unsure what to do with herself.

The sound of a knock sent her heart skyrocketing into her throat. She went to the door and looked through the peephole. No one.

A second knock, and she realized the noise came from behind her. An adjacent room. She swallowed an insane laugh. Of course she wasn't really alone.

She pasted a stern face on, and went to answer. Her giggle slipped out when she saw Blake on the other side, and she bit back the sound before it could become a cackle. "In room babysitter?" she asked.

"No. It sucks, doesn't it?" he asked.

"What does?"

"Always second-guessing everyone. Looking behind every corner for the deception. The conspiracy."

She let him in and locked the door behind him, then leaned back against it, arms crossed. She was struggling with the odd chasm that lay between being surrounded by too many people, and not wanting to be alone. "Aren't you used to it by now?"

"No. I don't think I ever will be." His tone was an odd cocktail of sorrow, bitterness, and regret. His phone rang, and he held a finger to his lips, to indicate she should be quiet.

"Allen," he barked into the device. "Yeah, I got her… I'll take first shift tonight… Damn straight it is. Make sure you have someone here to relieve me promptly at eight… Sure. See you then."

He looked at Reagan after he disconnected. "I'm sorry about that. I just wanted to let you know I checked the room, it's why I had Gale give you this one. There are no cameras or mics. The place is yours, secure and safe. I'll leave you alone now."

"Wait." She grabbed his wrist before she

could think about what she was doing. Darkness closed in on her mind at the thought of being left alone in a tiny room. "You don't have to go yet. I mean, you're staying next door anyway, right? They trust you to watch me? It won't hurt anything if you stay a couple more minutes? I mean, unless you need to go." She clenched her jaw to stop her rambling.

He pulled a chair out. "I can stay."

She reclaimed her spot on the bed. Great. Now that he was here, she didn't have anything to say. If she asked him about who he was, would he answer?

"How long have you been doing this? You said seven years with"—she stopped herself from saying *Hare*; that was still her secret— "Jabberwock. But before that?"

"I came from…" He shook his head. "Doesn't matter. I'd planned to enlist for as long as I can remember. I was going to be a Marine, damn it. The towers fell when I was sixteen, and that reinforced my decision. It gets a little muddy from there, but tests, aptitude, education, and I landed here. I have a knack for blending into my environment."

"Is this a Grosse Point Blank kind of thing?" She tried to keep the teasing in her voice. To prevent things from dipping into the realm of too serious. "You lacked a certain moral compass?"

His laugh was dry. "There are days I wish that was true. It would make a lot of this easier." He shook his head. "Anyway, when Jabberwock popped onto the radar, they needed agents with enough technical skill to talk the talk, and people skills.

About a dozen of us fit the bill. They altered our pasts and sent us in. I climbed fastest and highest, especially after… I'm saying too much."

She wouldn't fill in the blank for him. She had a feeling it sounded like, *Especially after Jabberwock lost one of his generals and needed a replacement.* Alex's role was another secret she'd keep, if he didn't already know. "I get it. *Don't trust anyone.* Right?"

"Exactly." He leaned forward and rested his elbows on his knees, as he stared straight ahead.

She had a feeling she wouldn't see the same things he did, if she followed his line of sight. Was this what Alex went through? Hare said Alex enjoyed his work. Was that true, or was it a mask, like Blake wore? "It must make it difficult to connect with anyone."

"It does." He let out a shaky sigh and looked at her. "You said you started pursuing Jabberwock because of your brother. What happened there?"

"You really don't know?"

He shook his head. "We pulled your files when you approached Wayne. I knew you had a brother and that he passed away about five years ago. His records were a little odd."

"Odd how?" She'd never seen any discrepancies. Then again, she didn't spend much time digging into Alex's past, because she thought she knew it.

"They looked a lot like mine. No digital photos. No passport. No state ID. Like I told you before, we assumed there was a connection, but didn't have confirmation."

Even with the power of thousands of people behind them, they never found more than Reagan did. She felt a little smug about that. "He'd told me a few times he worked for this guy. This Jabberwock. Then he told me one day he was in trouble, and that was the last time I heard from him."

Hare's story surged back, lies mixed with truth, hammering in her skull. She pressed her palms to her eyes until she saw stars, and tried to focus on that.

"Hey." Blake's voice and the warmth of his hand on her arm dragged her back. "I'm sorry." He'd said that a lot over the past couple of days.

It bothered her that she believed he was sincere. "Thanks."

"I'm giving you all this information about me, and I think that's the first real thing you've told me about you."

"You know everything about me. *My* public past hasn't been doctored, and you've been watching me for a minimum of six months."

"But none of that tells me who you are." He trailed his hand down her arm to grasp her fingers. "And before you counter and deflect—which you will—yes, I really want to know."

"Why?"

"On paper, you're statistically interesting. High IQ. Interesting degree choices. Impressive job prospects. But meeting you in person was different. In Vegas, I really was there to keep you safe. Wayne had been working with us for a while. You came along, and you had a new perspective that opened a lot of new avenues for us. Every time he panicked, we listened. That night, he insisted we put someone on you personally. I was already in town, and if you were with me, anyone who came looking for you from Jabberwock's organization would think I'd gotten to you first."

Except that wasn't the case. It would have blown his cover. No reason to dwell on that now, despite the whisper of guilt she felt about being the one to spill the beans. "The sex?"

"You weren't shy about being interested, and it was incredible. But you caught my attention as you. I'm... uh... a bit hooked now. I want to know more, and not for professional reasons."

He's almost as stuck in this as I am. The realization slammed into her. She didn't want to feel sympathy for him. Demonizing the enemy made it easier to keep them at arm's length, and he was as much the enemy as anyone. Wasn't he? His lies were reasonable, given his job, and he seemed genuinely upset about the way she'd been treated.

Would it hurt to trust one person?

Yes.

Chapter Nineteen

A yawn interrupted Regan's internal argument, splitting her jaw and making her eyes water.

"When was the last time you slept? As in, *really* slept?" Blake asked.

"How long ago was Las Vegas?"

"Wow. Okay, you need rest." He stood and tugged her to her feet. "I'll leave you to sleep. No one is going to wake you up or assault you with noise, and the curtains block a lot of light. I'll be next door if you need me."

She gripped his fingers tighter when he tried to pull away, and an irrational surge of panic built inside. "No."

"What's wrong?"

Everything, but that didn't explain what she was doing. "I don't want to sleep alone. I don't mean like sex or anything. But don't leave me in here by myself and walk out the door." She was being stupid and childish, and she couldn't help herself.

"Okay." His simple reply chased creeping shadows to the back of her mind, and the fist around her lungs loosened. "Door stays open, and I stay with you."

She nodded, not having a response or trusting herself to speak.

He pointed her toward the bed. "Shoes and jeans off."

She hesitated. Which didn't make any sense. He'd seen her naked.

"So you're comfortable." He unbuttoned his shirt and draped it over the back of a nearby chair, took off his socks and shoes to set aside, and shed his slacks. He pulled back the comforter. "You need sleep. Come on."

"Okay." She stripped down to her T-shirt and panties, and climbed into the bed.

The moment he lay next to her, she curled up against his chest. She hated how safe this felt, but when he wrapped an arm around her, more of the shadows receded.

He trailed his fingers through her hair, and she allowed herself to fall into the comfort. She was grateful he didn't say anything else. It was going to be hard enough to sleep as it was.

"Reagan." A male voice slammed through her dreams. She forced her eyes open, and a jumble of images assaulted her mind, overlapping the unfamiliar room. She jolted up and scooted away until her back hit the wall.

"It's just me." Blake stood nearby, watching her. He was already dressed.

She gave a nervous laugh. "I know." She climbed from the bed and pulled her jeans on.

"You can go back to sleep if you want, but I wanted to let you know I was leaving before the next guy comes in to replace me for the morning."

Reality sank back in, lowering her heart rate with it. She wanted to crawl under the covers and stay there for a hundred years. Besides the abrupt awakening, she'd slept better than in ages.

"The room is yours for as long as you need it, but I don't know how long it will be until I can work myself back into the rotation of being here at night. I'll try and make sure that whoever is next door gives you space."

She nodded.

He kissed her on the forehead. "I'll see you as soon as I can."

After he left, and she dressed, she stood in the room for several minutes, paralyzed with doubt. She forced courage through her veins, rebuilt the walls around her, and walked into the hallway. There was a woman in a bathrobe, a few doors down, bending to fetch her paper.

"Morning." Reagan flashed her a friendly smile.

The woman waved.

She could do this. Walk out of the hotel. Take her tail with her.

She spent most of her day like the one before—wandering town near the grocery store where she'd received the wire transfer, in hopes one of Hare's people would approach her. If she didn't get a nibble today, she'd send out a stronger signal tomorrow.

When six rolled around, she was starting to

think she needed to do exactly that. She returned to the same Chinese restaurant for dinner. She knew the layout of the place, so it was as close to reassuring as she could get.

She took a seat at the crowded bar. As people left and new patrons arrived, she kept her head down, despite the urge to examine every face. If her company was looking for her, seeing them coming wouldn't do her any good, and she didn't know what anyone looked like anyway. Not Jabberwock's or Blake's people

The seat to her right was vacated. Less than five minutes later, someone else slipped in.

"You here alone, gorgeous?" Dormouse's familiar voice—one that would both haunt and take point as the hero in her dreams for a long time—almost shattered Reagan's chill.

Reagan didn't twitch, despite the pounding of her heart. "I'm waiting for friends, but they're running late." She hoped the words were seen as a warning rather than a threat.

"Buy you a drink while you wait? I've been told I'm good company."

Reagan risked a glance. She didn't recognize Dormouse, which was probably the point. The other woman wore large glasses that distorted her cheeks and eyes, and her hair was black and hung in loose ringlets down her back. She was dressed in a faded concert T-shirt and denim skirt.

"A drink sounds good. Dirty martini," Reagan said. Not knowing who was watching her now or how much they could hear, she felt unsafe have an conversation out here. She needed an excuse to pull Dormouse away.

Dormouse waved the bartender over and ordered the drinks. Even dressed down, each movement she made was smooth and refined, as if she knew the world was watching.

Reagan wanted to learn how to do that. Another time, of course.

"I don't think I've seen you in here before." Dormouse's tone was casual.

"I haven't been in town long. Still figuring out the lay of the land and such."

Their drinks were served, and Reagan reached for hers. She caught the stem on her fingers and dumped the martini into her lap. "Shit." She jumped back from her seat, shaking liquid from her hands.

"Clumsy. That's cute." Dormouse grabbed a wad of napkins and dabbed up some of the excess.

Reagan scowled. "I need to wash some of this off."

"I'll help."

The moment they were in the bathroom, Dormouse backed her against the far wall, near the door going who-knew-where. With only three stalls in the place, a quick glance was enough to show they were alone.

"How long do you have?" Dormouse whispered in her ear. She gripped Reagan's hips, and pressed close. If anyone walked in on them, they'd look like they were making out.

"I don't know." Reagan shook her head. "Two minutes? Thirty seconds?"

"No one from Wonderland is supposed to

approach you except me. Where have you been?"

"I'm only telling Hare."

Dormouse nipped her neck hard enough it stung. "Not happening."

"Tell him I haven't spilled his secret."

"If you mean about Hatter, the word is out, and he's vanished."

If only they knew. Hare would, soon enough. Reagan couldn't ignore the twinge of guilt at the thought of the betrayal—playing one against the other for her shot at freedom. "Not that secret. One no one else knows. One Jabberwock wants kept safe."

"Bullshit." Dormouse stepped back. "Where does this door go?"

"I'm not sure. I saw the video." She didn't know why she mentioned it. The damn thing haunted her every time she let it back into her head.

Dormouse paled. "Of what?"

"The rape. Your execution. I wanted to applaud you, especially after I was forced to watch it more times than I can count."

"Where have you been?" Dormouse asked again.

This was a dangerous bluff, but Reagan had to take it, in order for things to come together her way. "I'm only telling Hare."

"Miss, are you all right in there?" A male voice carried through the main door.

Dormouse shook her head and took her chances with the rear exit.

Less than a second after she vanished, the bathroom door slammed open, and two men in suits burst in, guns drawn. A third stood to the side.

"On the ground, *now*," another man ordered. "Hands behind your head." He nodded at the spot Dormouse had disappeared through.

As Reagan followed their commands without question, she prayed the other woman was long gone.

Guy number three left to find Dormouse, and one of the remaining suits cuffed Reagan, then hauled her to her feet. They were only a hair gentler than last time.

Guy-Three returned a moment later, shaking his head. "The other one is gone. Who were you talking to?" He growled.

Reagan shrugged. "My new girlfriend. Amazing kisser. I'm thinking it's time to switch teams." She didn't feel any of the bravado she projected. Her pulse galloped, and she was surprised she didn't piss herself.

The suit who cuffed her jerked her arm, grinding against the burns hidden under long sleeves.

She couldn't fight her whimper. Protesting wouldn't do her any good. Even if she screamed, and someone called the cops, and the video went viral, it didn't mean anyone would ever see her again.

One of the suits with a gun said, "Let's get her out of here." He and his buddy holstered their weapons, and Guy-Three threw his jacket over Reagan's shoulders, covering her cuffed hands.

They surrounded her as they escorted her from the restaurant.

There was no blindfold this time. The drive was short and took them to a local police station. They tossed her in a room with a mirror, attached her cuffs to a bolt on the table, and walked out.

The moment they were gone, she looked straight at the glass, and in a voice as steady as possible, said, "This is a bad way to do this."

Chapter Twenty

When Blake joined her in the room, his glare shredded her from the inside out. She didn't want this to impact him, but there was no choice. Not that it mattered, since she was planning to let he and Hare take each other on. He looked like he'd aged ten years since this morning, with the shadows under his eyes, his ruffled hair, and a day's worth of scruff on his chin.

"You can't pull bullshit like this." His voice was sharp.

"Like what? I thought I was being given space to do this thing." She tried to look casual and apathetic, but guilt wormed its way out.

He growled. "No, you didn't think that."

"It was worth it."

"Not if we haul you out of here tonight."

Panic surged through her, and she bit back a plea. He winced. She must not be hiding her doubt as well as she wanted.

"I can get you what you want," she said.

"Jabberwock."

Technically, yes. "No. Dormouse and Hare."

He pulled out the chair across from her and dropped into it heavily. "We could have had them anytime. That's not a tempting offer, and if it's all you've got, your deal is off."

"But you make them vanish, and Jabberwock has lost all three generals like that."

"You don't think he's got people waiting in the wings?" Blake asked. "My money says he's already got someone pegged to be Gryphon."

"I think, if the two of them go MIA after talking to me, and based on your recent departure, he won't know where they've gone or why. He'll wonder if the other two have turned on him, and who else he can't trust. That means going on alert. Closing ranks. Making mistakes." It wouldn't work that way, because of who Jabberwock was, but she was running out of ways to cling to her freedom.

He stared at her for several seconds, searching her face, mouth twisted in a scowl.

If she didn't think they had an audience, she'd drop the false bravado. Beg him to please understand.

Instead, she stared back, wishing she could convey something with her eyes.

He stood, leaned over the table, and unlocked her cuffs. "You've used up your strikes."

"That's what you said last time."

"I'm not leaving your side until this is over."

She shook her head. "You want Hare to come to me? I can't be seen with you."

"You're about to walk out of a police station, having only been held for a few hours, after meeting with—let me guess—Dormouse?"

So much for the clever disguise. Then again, Hatter probably knew Dormouse better than most people did. "Yes."

"She's going to know you've got some sort of deal going on," Blake said.

Don't change your mind now. Let me go. Too bad she didn't have Force powers. "She already does, but she doesn't have details, and she wants them. I told her I'd only share with Hare. If he's going to approach, he won't do it with you there." Actually, she didn't know that. Hare was a difficult man to second-guess. He might like the challenge of Hatter being by her side.

Or he might blow a gasket and kill them both. She hated that she couldn't anticipate those odds. She'd feel safer staying with Hatter until this was all over, but it was too big a risk. "I should get going."

He frowned and gestured at the mirror. A second later, there was a buzz, and he opened the door.

Would she see him back in her room any time soon? She hoped so. It was a dangerous thing to wish for, but she wanted that illusion of security wherever she could find it.

She didn't dare interact with him in any significant way, to find out when he might be guarding her again, while other people were watching. "See you next time they bring me in?"

"I'm going home to crash as soon as I'm done here, and I'm off for the next week. Someone else on my team can bail you out tomorrow if you do this again."

So much for this being her final strike. She

could wait a week to see him again, as long as Hare didn't get to her first.

An ache pinged in her chest at the thought this might be the last time she ever talked to Blake. How long until her luck ran out with this insane plan to use her knowledge of Jabberwock's identity to buy her freedom?

A few minutes later, she walked out of the police station. If nothing else, it was nice to not spend a night in a cell. It was almost midnight. What was she supposed to do, to pass the time, and how antsy would her tails get if she didn't go back to her hotel?

Seeking out Blake felt like putting them both at too high a risk.

Someone slammed into her, knocking her back and sending her sprawling to the cement.

"Sorry. So sorry." Someone offered Reagan a hand up.

Reagan looked up, and recognition spread through her. *Ten of Diamonds.*

Ten winked. "Gotta run. Sorry again," she called over her shoulder as she jogged into the night.

That was so suspicious. The problem was, Reagan didn't know what she was supposed to take from the encounter. Was that a warning? A brush-off? Something else?

She went back to her hotel. She didn't sleep, and she spent the next day inside. It made her itch to be confined to the small room, but she told herself it was her choice.

Around dinner, she emerged. If Hare was going to approach her, he'd wait until he thought he was safe. She had no idea if that would happen tonight.

She skipped the Chinese restaurant tonight and found a diner instead. A place she could sit for a couple of hours and drink coffee, and not look suspicious doing so.

By the time eight rolled around, she thought she might jitter out of her skin. Maybe she should have skipped that last cup.

She went back to her hotel and waited. No Blake. No Hare.

The next several days were a repeat, with the except that each passing out cranked her anxiety up another notch. She wasn't sure how long she could hold out if this kept up.

By day six she thought she might tear her hair out. Day seven, when someone knocked on the door joining her room to the next, she wanted to praise whatever God heard her. It didn't matter who it was, as long as she was doing something different.

She answered, and the moment she saw Blake, stepped aside. Relief spilled through her.

"You're playing a dangerous game. Do you realize that?" His tone was kind, despite the gruff greeting.

She didn't, at first. It took much longer to sink in than it should have. It was pretty difficult to ignore now. "Yes."

"I'm glad you're all right." He took the same seat he had the other night, undid the top button on his shirt, and loosened his tie. "You are, aren't you?"

"All right? I think so." Part of her wanted the comfort of the other night, and more of her wanted to erase all her thoughts. Replace them with something more visceral.

She settled for keeping her distance.

He studied her. "I won't bite."

"Not even if I beg?" That wasn't what she meant to say.

"Come here."

She crossed the room. When she drew close, he grabbed her wrist and pulled her into his lap.

The abrupt gesture startled her.

"Is this better?" he asked.

It shouldn't be. So help her, it was a really bad idea given how much she enjoyed the security and assumption of it. "Yes."

"Good." He placed a finger under her chin and turned her face toward his. His kiss was a brush of feathers across her lips and ended too soon. "I missed you. That's probably fucked up, but it is what it is."

"Then we're fucked up together." She leaned in, to rest her head against him. At this angle, ear pressed to his neck, she heard the rapid thrum of his pulse. Given everything she'd been through, this didn't seem like a smart attachment to make. He'd lied as much as anyone. Was as much a part of this mess. Would be gone the moment she broke away.

That didn't mean she couldn't enjoy the closeness tonight.

"You scare me." He trailed his fingers through her hair. "In so many ways. Also, I liked you better as a redhead."

"Blonde wasn't my choice." And in few days, she'd probably be a brunette. She refused to read anything into his other comment.

His chest rose and fell beneath her, the steady rhythm soothing fractured nerves. "There's no scenario here where you walk free. Not any that Homeland Security or Jabberwock envisions." Blake's voice was sad. "You've figured that out, haven't you?"

"Yes."

"And you can't run while they're watching you."

"No." She wouldn't spill her plan. It was hers. The key to getting away. Not to safety—she'd be looking over her shoulder for a long time—but to being out from under anyone else's constant gaze and control.

He nudged her forward so he could look her in the eye. "What are you up to, Alice?"

The nickname didn't bother her tonight. The affection behind it was sincere. It would be easier to do what she had in mind with him. Someone who had experience vanishing off the grid. Who had information about how both operations worked. *Fuck it.* That was her, trying to rationalize. She didn't want to leave Blake behind. The thought wasn't reasonable, but that didn't make it easier for her to unthink it.

"If you're running, I'm going with you," he said.

Yes. Okay. Let's go now. We can ditch your friends, can't we? "Why?"

"Because I'm sick of this game. Playing both sides… I can't do that again, and I can't go back to field work or a desk job, especially the kind of shit detail they'll give me if I lose you. But that's all secondary. I care about you. It's been a long time since anything meant more than going through the motions."

She didn't know what to do with the confession. It wasn't as though he'd said he loved her. She didn't even think he was holding something like that back, though it might become love if they stuck together.

What if this is a trap? Their way of finding out what I'm really up to? Then she was done. If this was how they got their information, she couldn't play or second-guess anymore. Every step of the way from here on out would be risk filled. This was another one of those instances.

"Yes," she said.

He cupped her face between his palms and kissed her hard. A thread of desperation lay underneath, intertwining with security. She dug her fingers into his chest and kissed back, memorizing the moment. The way two days of beard scuffed her chin. The cotton under her fingertips. His scent, clean and spicy, and the tick of the clock on the wall, dancing with the traffic outside.

She shifted her position to get a better angle, and he grew hard underneath her. He slid one hand to the back of her neck. His calloused fingers on her sensitive skin sent tingles dancing over her. She wanted this moment to last forever. It was safe here. She knew the rules. She liked the other player.

When they broke apart, her lips were tender and swollen. He traced a finger over the bottom one. Affection shone in his eyes in the low light.

"I was top of my graduating class, you

know." His words barely reached her ears.

"Oh yeah?"

He nodded. "And I've seen your IQ scores. Your entrance exams."

"I feel like you're about to make a point, and this isn't as random and un-sexy a tangent as it sounds."

"I am, in fact." He tangled his fingers with hers. "We're about to do something really stupid, for two people who are supposed to be smart."

She shook her head. "We already did the stupid stuff. Now, we make the best of it."

"Did you know, if you pay the desk clerk the right amount of money, you can get a key to any adjoining room in this place? I bet you did." Hare's voice shattered the mood and spilled ice over her. "Sorry. Bad timing on my part?"

Chapter Twenty-One

"You two make an adorable couple." Hare's tone was conversational and friendly. "I'm a little hurt, though, Reagan. I was hoping you and I had that spark. I thought we had something."

She felt Blake's muscles shift and tense, as is he were ready to strike. He adjusted himself, sliding one hand between them, and to his holster. It must be killing him to have his back to Hare.

She gritted her teeth and tried to ignore the bit of her that had liked what she had with Hare. Physical. Simple. Intense. If she'd been nudged a little further over the edge, it wouldn't have taken much for him to persuade her to side with him rather than Blake. *Persuade* was a horrible word to use, but Hare never gave her real choices. He did a marvelous job of painting her into a corner and making his preference appear to be the only attractive way out.

"Nothing?" Hare raised his brows. "No witty comeback or stammering cry of disbelief?"

"If you're going to be all cliché-super-villain, I refuse to ask, *how did you find us*?" Reagan said.

Hare shrugged. "I'll tell you anyway. For

Hatter's benefit, so he doesn't make the same mistake again. He used his knowledge and contacts at this place to hook you up. Once I knew you were still in town, I had a list within a few hours of his local contacts as Hatter. You, Reagan, tipped your hand about where you were. Ten saw him leave the same police station you were being held in. *Bam.* Someone followed you here, told me which room you were in, and I alakazam, here I am."

He pulled his gun from its holster with a single fluid motion. "Stand up. The two of you make me nervous."

Reagan's hammering heart sped up as he pointed the pistol at them. As Blake helped her shift off his lap, he drew his sidearm. As they stood, he pointed it at Hare.

"Hmm… Did you realize that was just a Glock in his pocket?" Hare asked. "I don't like two-to-one odds, but I don't think they're balanced the way Hatter expects." He pointed his pistol at Reagan. "I have it on good authority you haven't shared Jabberwock's secret."

She couldn't keep her hands from shaking, as she looked down the barrel of the gun. "I haven't. I'm keeping his as well." She nodded at Blake.

Blake shifted his posture, arm going rigid.

"Uh-uh," Hare chided him and pulled back the hammer on his gun, gaze never leaving Reagan. "I know you're good, Blake—better than me—I saw your files from the Marines before we erased your past. If you finger twitches, I won't wait to see if you pull the trigger, I'll shoot her."

Reagan swallowed. Hare was nuts enough

he'd make good on the threat just for kicks. "We're talking. We're good. We all have secrets, remember?"

"Why did you keep mine?" Hare asked.

"They're not my secrets to share."

Hare raised his brows. "How altruistic of you. Then it's not because you hope to use one or both as a bargaining chip."

Her gut sank. "Maybe."

"You're clever." Hare smirked. "You could have been my White Queen, you know."

"No thanks." Reagan shook her head. "I'd hate to break the *no other royalty in the court* rule."

"Are we doing something or having a tea party?" Blake asked.

Hare's grin grew. "You remember how this game is played. That makes me happy. I'm tempted to gut you right now, for lying to me. I gave Reagan's brother a good death. Quick. Dignified. But what I'd like to do to you..."

"Enough." Reagan wanted this over with. She'd had a ticking clock over her head for too long. Regardless of the outcome here, she wanted to move on. "I'm bargaining, remember?"

Hare nodded. "With my secret, yes. I don't like that. Let's shift the playing field. You tell me Hatter's secret and him mine, and I'll tell you one he's kept from you."

She glanced at Blake. "I know his secrets." Doubt crept into her voice.

"I doubt that." Hare never relaxed his aim at her.

Of course there were things she didn't know

about Blake. She expected that. Could she sit through Hare reciting a list of Hatter's kills? The deals he'd done? She'd have to find out either way. She'd rather know now, than later. "All right. Sharing time. Who goes first?"

"Eenie… meenie… minie…" Hare chanted. "*Oh*. I'll tell Hatter *my* secret. Sound good?"

"Alice?" Blake looked at her.

Hare snorted. "I'm not even touching that one."

"Fine," Reagan said. This thing was crumbling. It barely resembled her plan. She was supposed to say she'd keep Hare's secret, in exchange for him letting them walk. That he could come after her the moment she told someone. Now that she thought through it, it was the most delusional idea she'd come up with in the last few weeks, and that was saying a lot.

Hare mimed tipping an invisible hat, never lowering his gaze or gun. "I'm Jabberwock. Pleased to meet you."

"No." Blake clenched his jaw. "What were you really going to tell me?"

She cringed at his hurt and disbelief. "That's it. Hare is Jabberwock. I'm sorry I kept it to myself. If the people you work for knew, I'd be fucked."

Telling Blake's employers what she knew meant things like witness protection and always hiding from whoever Jabberwock left behind—if he was even convicted. They'd searched for years and had no idea he hid right under their noses. The Feds couldn't keep her safe.

Which was why she gambled on Jabberwock.

If he could hide himself, he could hide her. Or kill her, but that was a possibility either way. This gave her better odds.

"There's witness protection. A new life. Starting over." Blake ticked off on his fingers.

"Which we're doing anyway?" She couldn't keep the desperation from her voice.

He frowned.

"Who *does* he work for?" Hare interrupted. "That's his secret, am I right? The one you have for me?"

Blake glared at him. "I'm NSA. I'm working with Homeland Security. It's a collaborative effort."

Hare's eyes grew wide. "Wow. I have multiple agencies on my tail. Why do you people care about me?"

"You've committed acts of cyber terrorism." Blake hesitated. "Well, not committed, but you're tied to them. Conspiracy."

How were their arms not aching by now? It was a ridiculous thought, but the whole situation was surreal.

Hare looked at her again. "Here's the thing about me. About *us*. The thing Hatter probably didn't tell you. Ninety-nine percent of the time, I'm a facilitator. Nothing more. If someone needs something, they come to me, and I put them in touch with the person who has it. It's rare for me to pull the trigger."

"I'm glad Alex was the exception." She let the hurt ooze into her words. "I'm not discussing with you the morality of being a middle man, versus doing the work yourself."

"That's okay." Hare waved his gun erratically. It was more fear-inducing than him keeping it level. "Your secret about Hatter isn't very good. Especially not compared to what he got to learn, so I'll tell you what I know about him instead."

Reagan looked at Blake. It couldn't be any worse than her hiding Jabberwock's identity. *You sure about that?* "I'm listening."

Blake's scowl deepened.

"That night in Vegas?" Hare said. "*Blake* wasn't there to keep you safe. I had no idea where you were, and he knew that. I didn't care what you were doing with Wayne Dickinson, because you and he weren't a threat. I kept loose tabs on you, for Alex, but you were background noise."

"Bullshit." Blake spat the word. "You rearranged everything to grab her when Wayne died."

"*Wrong.*" Hare made a buzzing noise, and Reagan jumped. "I rearranged everything to nab *you*, Blake. I went to Dr. Dickinson's funeral to check on White Rabbit's little sister. Maybe buy her lunch, meet the girl her brother adored, and see if she could give me any information about why someone would off her instructor. Your people shot at her."

Reagan's stomach lurched. She knew the gunman was a Fed. Blake told her that. But at the time, she'd glossed over the news in favor of more pressing matters.

"So you just happened to be at the right place, at the right time?" A sneer cut through Blake's voice.

"Yup," Hare said. "Luckily for her."

Pieces clicked in Reagan's head, and she

swallowed back the nausea. She looked at Blake. "Your people killed Wayne. You weren't in Las Vegas to keep me safe. You were there to make sure I didn't change my mind about going home early."

Blake clenched his jaw.

The lack of denial was enough confirmation for her. "I was going to tell you about Jabberwock. Did you ever plan to bring this up about Wayne?"

"Of course. We haven't had a lot of time to talk."

Reagan looked at Hare. She'd deal with that later. Once she and Blake were gone. *If I go with him.* Which she would. "Great. Swell. Shiny. Everyone knows everything about everyone else. Do I still get to bargain?"

"You don't have any chips left," Hare said.

"I didn't tell anyone else. Only Blake knows, and he's not going back to work." Reagan dug through her thoughts, burrowing behind every corner to find a new solution.

"Well, no. He's not. Not if the two of you are dead." Hare leveled his gun at her.

That was it. Reagan grasped, desperate for something. "There's no game in that."

Hare raised his brows. "What makes you think I care?"

"Because I spent time around you. You dropped hints about your identity. You twisted things around, to see what I'd do next. You didn't want me to figure out who you were so you could prove I was a clever girl. You did it for the game." That glimmer of madness he radiated would also have an impact on his decision.

"Maybe a little." Hare's smirk returned. "What's this new game of yours?"

"Let us walk out of here." Reagan needed this to work. More than anything ever. "Give us a head start. Take us off federal radar and make us vanish digitally."

"That doesn't sound like a very fun game." Hare furrowed his brow.

She held up her hand. "I'm not done. When a week is up, come after us."

Hare seemed to consider this. "That gives you enough time to hide far far away. Drop off the face of the planet. To grow old and happy together."

"No." Reagan corrected him. "That is—of course we'll hide. We'd be stupid not to. But I'm going to dismantle your organization a piece at a time. Take it apart until your epic Wonderland is burned and twisted and crumbling around you. While you try to stop me."

"*What?*" Blake raised his voice. "That's not the plan. Why don't I shoot him?"

Hare *tsk*ed. "Reagan will tell you. It's her proposal."

"Well?" Blake glanced at her, before returning his attention to Hare.

"Everyone in Wonderland knows who we are. I'd prefer to only have one target on my back. The appeal to Hare in erasing us from public records is the Feds don't step on his toes. If we kill him and run, everyone chases us. If we kill him and go the legal route, there's that whole issue of keeping us safe again. I trust me more than the people Blake works for."

"We were going to run anyway," Blake argued.

Reagan agreed. "Maybe I'm being paranoid. Looking for shadows where there aren't any. Can't possibly think what in my recent experience could cause that." She let the sarcasm drip from her words. "But we weren't going to piss off someone like Dormouse first."

"I wish I had a good counter for that," Blake said.

Hare chuckled and tossed her a pair of car keys. "There's a white Accord in E4. When you leave the room, take the east stairwell. No one will see you. If you exit through the parking garage heading south, you're clear for at least a few blocks. As long as no one recognizes you, you're clear a lot longer than that."

"And you're just going to let us walk?" Blake asked.

Hare holstered his gun and held up his hands. "That's what we discussed. You'll need to learn to pay attention."

Blake leveled his pistol at Hare again. Reagan pushed his arms down. "We need to go," she said. "

He looked at Hare one last time, then holstered his weapon. When he headed into the adjoining room, he bumped Hare's shoulder hard enough to jar him.

Hare didn't flinch.

Blake returned a moment later and handed Regan a button-down shirt and a baseball cap. "Pull your hair up," he said.

"Why do you have things like this in there?" she asked as she stripped off her T-shirt and tugged on the button-down, ignoring Hare's smirk and appraising gaze. She wrapped her hair up and tucked it under the hat, then pulled the brim low.

"In case one of our guys wants a change of appearance when he follows you." Blake changed into a T-shirt and jeans and another hat. He grasped Reagan's hand and tugged her toward the door.

"See you in a week, Alice," Hare called as they left.

Blake and Reagan followed Hare's instructions. The car was where he said. She let Blake drive and kept an eye on the mirrors. Neither of them said much beyond navigation checks. When they were about an hour outside the city, he stopped at an ATM and withdrew the maximum cash limit from a series of credit cards.

"Aren't you worried about being traced?" she asked.

He put half the cash in his wallet, handed her the rest, and pulled back onto the freeway. "It doesn't matter. We're not staying here."

"What's this for?" She couldn't keep the surprise from her voice.

"Just in case."

"This is a lot of money to trust me with."

"But that's the thing. I *do* trust you. The last seven years of my life are gone. I have to put my faith in someone, in order to survive, and we're in this together."

"But... what about what I kept from you?" She thought about Wayne. How she'd blamed

Jabberwock all this time. How she had no idea about the truth, partly because she'd been blind to other options.

"About Jabberwock being Hare? I know why you did it. I get it." He squeezed her hand. "You had valid reasons."

"Yeah." The problem was, she didn't feel the same about what he'd kept from her.

He glanced at her. "Are you all right?"

"Better than in a long time." The doubt she felt was a product of shock. Once she had a chance to process all this information, she'd be okay. Blake had a point—she had to trust someone.

"Why did they kill Wayne?" She couldn't let this drop after all. It was such a key thing. At the center of this whole mess, and the one answer she didn't have.

Blake sighed. In the passing streetlamps, he looked as tired as she felt. "He became a threat. His paranoia hit the point where they—my superiors, I didn't make decisions like that—felt he needed to go."

"Wow." Reagan dragged out a shaky breath. She didn't know how to process that. Apparently pulling the trigger was simple no matter which side someone was on. It made her decision to walk away from it all feel that much more right. "And me? I saw you at the funeral."

The way he scrubbed his face elongated the shadows under his eyes. "I was there to extract you. When you were seen with Hare, the decision changed. When Jabberwock took you under his wing, the decision changed again. Like I said before—they thought he was moving heaven and earth for you."

"Joke's on them." She laughed bitterly.

Silence descended over the car except for discussion about their travel plans. They could head north, but while he had other passports, Reagan didn't. They headed southeast instead.

A few hours later, they pulled into a gas station. He set the car to fill up, then poked his head in her window. "I'm going to grab us some snacks."

She gave him a tired smile. "I'll be in the restroom. Give me a few minutes." She watched him walk inside, and sick confusion swirled in her. She hated what she was about to do, but she didn't trust him.

Maybe that was on her, and maybe it was on him, but it didn't change how she felt. She grabbed the registration from the glove box, wrapped it around most of the money he'd given her, and set it on the driver's seat. She couldn't take all his cash, but she needed something. A couple hundred dollars would work.

She glanced at the gas station one last time, to make sure he was still occupied, then left the car and walked toward the rows of trucks on the other side of the lot. She scanned the faces of the smattering of drivers until she found someone who looked mostly harmless. Not that she was a good judge of what that meant, but she had to trust herself or she wouldn't be able to do this.

"Excuse me." She raced up to a woman climbing into the cab. "I'm…" She glanced over her shoulder, to make sure Blake wasn't following. "Can

I get a ride?"

The older woman eyed her with concern. "You okay, hon?"

"I just need to get out of here. Please?"

"Sure. Hop on in."

"Thank you." Reagan scrambled into the passenger seat.

She watched in the rear-view mirror as the gas station grew smaller and finally vanished. Was she doing the right thing? She was going to be asking that a lot, over the next few years. If she started off doubting herself now, she'd never survive.

She swallowed past the lump in her throat and looked at the road in front of them.

"I'm Tina. What's your name, hon?" The drive extended her hand in greeting.

Reagan accepted the handshake. "Alice."

"Where are you heading?"

"Anywhere that's not here."

Epilogue

Alice pushed back from the blackjack table and tossed the dealer a couple of chips. "I'm done. Thanks for the game." She was up about five grand. Easy to do on the high-roller tables. She'd had bigger wins, but the trick was to never get greedy when she counted cards. Lose a little, win a little, and spend enough on other games to keep her free suite and not be asked to leave.

She looked at the ceiling, spotted the nearest camera, and smiled, then headed for the cashiers' station. The simple action felt like ants crawling under her skin. She'd worked so hard to hide, and now she was exposing herself on purpose. To Jabberwock. *Please let him be in the mood for a game.* She said a second prayer that game would be letting her keep going, rather than some sort of psychological torment.

She handed her chips to a cashier. As she received her money, she looked up at the closest security camera. The elevators were her next stop.

It had been six months since she left Blake. Thinking about him still gnawed at her chest, but only if she let herself fall into that past. The first few weeks after, she struggled to get by. Two-hundred dollars didn't go far.

It was easier to stay off the grid than she thought, though. With no credit cards or ID, as long as she kept her head down and was nice to the right people, she could accomplish a lot.

She glanced at the camera on the lift ride up. It was nice to not have to wear the prosthetics today. They itched, but they made her face look like it had a different bone structure. The comfort didn't make up for the ill-ease clawing at her veins, begging her to stop this now.

Today, she needed to display her identity. The rational part of her mind hated being back in this world, but fury and the need to be the person in charge of her life overrode that. The time she spent in lockdown, and before that with Hare, she let someone else dictate the rules. And they didn't hesitate to manipulate and use her.

They'd done the same to Alex and Wayne, and fuck it if she refused to let that stand. Maybe some of Hare's madness had rubbed off on her, but she didn't care if that contributed to her motivation, as long as she saw this through.

The hallway to her room was empty. There were only a few suites up here. She strolled toward her door and pulled her card from her purse.

Someone wrapped their arms around her waist, and she recognized Hare's scent immediately. She hovered on a knife's edge between fear and revulsion. It took all her willpower not to jerk from his touch.

He brushed her ear with his lips and whispered, "The Lion and the Unicorn were fighting for the crown. The Lion chased the Unicorn all around town."

"Lion?" She turned to face him but didn't pull away. Her body molded to his, increasing her disgust another notch. "Another name?" she said. "How are you keeping track of them all?"

"You tell me, Alice."

She licked her bottom lip and gave him what she hoped was a wicked smile. "I'm glad you were here today."

"You're not very well hidden if you go places you expect to find me. And fleecing a casino owned by a business acquaintance of mine doesn't really live up to that threat you made last time we spoke."

"No. It really doesn't." She shifted against him, and nausea flickered inside when his cock hardened against her hip. She ignored her reaction. This was the game now.

She wouldn't have found him if it weren't for Alex's information. The photos Jabberwock himself made her take a second look at. The embedded code Alex left for her eyes only, that gave her insight into some of the organizations best kept secrets.

Jabberwock trailed his nose up the side of her neck. "I missed you." His phone buzzed.

"I can tell. You're vibrating with excitement."

He rolled his eyes, stepped back, and scanned his screen. "It's Queen of Hearts," he said without looking up.

"I thought you were the only royalty." She

didn't know why he shared, and the note certainly wasn't from the person she expected.

"I've tightened ranks, and Dormouse earned a promotion."

"Ah." Who she expected, after all. "Then we all have new names. What am I calling you?"

"It's not a secret anymore. I'm Jabberwock. *Fuck*." He looked at her. "Apparently, there's a virus on one of our servers. Only one. It's publishing a series of my IP addresses to the internet."

She widened her eyes and poured fake shock into her voice. "Oh my God. How horrible for you." She didn't expect him to flinch when he got the news of her first step toward her promise, but she did want to see his face. *Mission accomplished. Thank you for the tip from beyond the grave, big brother.*

"It's nothing that can't be fixed." He leaned in. He hovered his mouth over her lips. "Until next time." His breath fell across her skin.

She didn't miss that he dropped something in her purse, before he left.

She watched him walk away, then turned and headed in the other direction. Everything in her room could be replaced. Anything she needed, she carried on her. It was time to move to her next stop.

To be continued in *The Hatter and the Hare*...